Shadow Magic

Nazri Noor

This is a work of fiction. Similarities to real people, places, or events are entirely coincidental.

SHADOW MAGIC

First edition. June 6, 2018.

ISBN: 1719025053
ISBN-13: 978-1719025058

Chapter 1

The moon was my witness and accomplice as it cast shadows over the stuccoed walls of the hillside mansion. Long, deep shadows, perfect for hiding, for stepping into. I liked the darkness. It made my job easier: slip in, steal a witch's book of spells, and slip back out. No sweat. I breathed in the sweet night air up in the hills, the city of Valero's lights twinkling like stars in the valley below. It was a beautiful night for thieving.

You read that right. I definitely said book of spells. Or a grimoire, as we called them at the office. I should have clarified. My name is Dustin Graves, and I steal stuff for a living. Dust for short. Not the most flattering nickname, maybe, but it kind of says everything about what I can do. Which, I've been told, is nothing short of magic. Okay, real talk: it is magic. But we'll get to that.

The things I needed to steal? Arcane curiosities, mostly. Magical items, occult trinkets, sometimes, even ancient, powerful artifacts. Every assignment was different, depending on what the higher-ups at the Lorica asked me to fetch for them. Sometimes it was a piece of ensorcelled jewelry, one time, a gun modified to capture poltergeists. As a job, it was stimulating, challenging, and often totally dangerous. In short, I loved it.

See, there was a certain thrill to being a professional thief, this acknowledgement that I was being naughty and breaking rules on purpose. In fact, breaking into people's houses was a large part of my occupation. I should have been nervous that evening, by rights, but I'd done it enough times to know how it would all go down. Just another day on the job.

But I wasn't a criminal, oh no. Far from it. Sometimes people needed to be relieved of the dangerous relics they kept around the house. Sometimes people didn't realize that their fancy new earthenware pot was a shaman's soul jar, sealed and filled to the brim with the enraged spirits of their enemies.

I sifted around in my jacket's pocket, looking for the most important tool in my admittedly limited repertoire. It was only a little glass bottle, by all appearances, but it was inarguably my favorite of the gadgets that the Lorica provided for field work. I pulled out the stopper and held it up as close to the wall as I could without triggering the security system's sensors.

I loved this part. It was fascinating to listen for the faint crackle and the low hum as the phial began to fill with tiny bluish-white sparks that swirled, surged, then coalesced into miniature bolts of lightning. A storm in a bottle, so close you could taste the ozone and the electricity, all the power in the compound sucked neatly into this crystalline baby. And yes, that included the backup batteries for every camera, sensor, even the security system's main panel.

Folks back at the Lorica were always warning me about how it was important to handle the phial with extreme care, because of how it stored a lethal dose of electricity in such a fragile space. It was never a problem for me, though. The crystal was pretty sturdy, and it wasn't like I was ever dumb enough to hold it by the rim. There are lots of other less painful ways to die.

But yeah, life's been great since I became a Hound for the Lorica, thanks for asking. Exciting might be the right word. Maybe the stuff I did was a little riskier than I was used to – vacuuming electricity into a bottle teenier than a shot glass, doing my best not to trip security systems, one time even running from a pack of really, really pissed off dobermans. Still, I guess I was more inclined to take risks and try new things since I'd already been dead once before.

We'll get to that later. Promise. Because the actual magic comes next.

With the system out of the way, all that was left was to actually infiltrate the grounds, to slip into the house unseen and unheard. Some of my colleagues used cruder methods to gain access, whether with a set of lock picks or a carefully cut-out section of glass. Me? I got to use my magic, or the specific brand of it that I was good at.

I peered into the darkened house, picking out the right spot to enter. I didn't need a doorway or a window, mind you, just a pool of shadow big enough to fit my body. Sounds weird, I know, but I work with what I have, and what I have gets me work. The moonlight streaming in through the floor to ceiling windows cast a nicely sized shadow, just by a large potted plant.

Perfect. I rubbed my hands together and stepped into the shadow of the house on the patio outside. The cold of the night faded as my body shifted and slipped through the ethers. Once my skin began tingling with a faint warmth, I knew that I had made it inside the house. I emerged from the darkness, from the exact pool of shadow I'd selected over by the potted ficus. I patted myself down to check that I'd shadowstepped in one piece, and I smiled at the plant, as if in greeting.

I wish I could explain how it worked.

Shadowstepping was like teleportation, in some ways. I could move freely between two shadows, as long as they weren't that far apart: pop into one, then step out of the other. My magic had gotten me out of more jams than I have the time to tell you, and it was also the reason the Lorica kept me around. That, and because I was cute.

My boss Thea said that everyone at the Lorica had some natural aptitude for the arcane. Every mage was destined to polish their specialty – shadow magic, in my case – but it didn't mean that they couldn't expand their portfolio. It would take time, she said, and plenty of effort, but I might eventually learn how to shoot fire out of my bare hands, or even fly. Like a superhero, or a proper fantasy wizard. That sounded amazing.

Not every person should do magic, though, especially not the normals. That was the whole point of my job: to keep the really dangerous stuff out of inexperienced hands. A jewel that changed colors? Pretty and wondrous, sure, but mostly harmless. But a grimoire owned and personally penned by an eighteenth century French witch who left specific instructions on how to bring back the plague? No bueno.

Incidentally, that was the target for the night: an ancient book, ensconced somewhere in the confines of this enormous hillside Hollywood-wannabe mansion. According to the dossier I'd been given, the occupants were the Pruitts, a thirty-something couple who had made their killing off of reality television. The guy was a producer, the girl one of the stars. Yet even together, I was sure as anything that they couldn't make up even half of a competent sorcerer.

See, there's really no telling who's magical these days. I mean, it's California. You see a guy with a beard, a walking stick, and a pointy hat, he could just be a hipster, or maybe there's a cosplay convention in town. Not that Valero gets a lot of those, but you get my point. You never know when it comes to modern magic. That barista who makes a face every time you ask for almond milk in your latte could be a talented elementalist, just as the lady behind the counter at your local bodega could be a bruja.

But this couple? The Pruitts were nothing close to magical, and they just had to get their hands on a collector's item, this deadly-ass book of summoning. That was like the arcane equivalent of handing a pipe bomb to a toddler. The book belonged back at the Lorica, preferably wrapped in chains and placed under bulletproof glass and, like, a dozen spells of protection. The grimoire had to be removed, and I was the guy to make that happen. That was why the Lorica sent in their handsomest Hound.

From the vantage point of the potted plant I checked and checked again, making sure there wasn't some miniature pet dog I had missed. The poor little guys were adorable, genetic mishaps aside – adopt, people, don't support the shitty breeding industry – but they were yappy enough to wake their owners, and even small teeth could hurt like hell if the dog was agitated enough. Cats were even worse, little balls of fluff weaponized with tiny kitchen knives. I still had scars from a run-in with a Persian.

The coast was clear. The house had that minimalist yet somehow still ostentatious furniture you found in the homes of the rich and kind of famous, which limited my potential hiding spots, but it looked like I wouldn't have to resort to them anyway. There were no pets in sight, and no humans, either, which was arguably more important. That meant I could relax a little, take my time.

But just to be sure, I reached for another phial, this one filled with a glittery pink dust. Hell, for all I knew it could have been actual glitter, but Herald said it was perfect for covering my tracks. Not that I ever left any, mind, but better safe than sorry. I tapped some out onto the ground, grinding my shoes into the dust. The stuff disappeared into my soles, supposedly making it even easier for me to move around without making any noise. Sure, why not. A little bit of fairy dust to help Dust out.

I crept forward, taking care not to make a peep because, magical assistance or no, it wasn't like I was invisible. I craned my neck in search of the witch's grimoire, sure that the Pruitts had stashed it away in a highly secure safe or somewhere similar, when I noticed the sound of rustling, like something fluttering, only more dry and, well, papery. Ah, there it was, right on the marble kitchen counter, laid open and flat: The Book of Plagues. How anticlimactic.

It was just as the Lorica had described, nearly a foot in length, the approximate thickness of a phonebook, and bound in a deep red leather. Demon skin, if my dossier was to be believed, though I was never quick to discount little tidbits like that anymore.

Some of the Hands at the Lorica had told me about their experiences with demons, enough to tell me that I'd never want to run into one, and enough to tell me that the witch who handmade this grisly book of shadows was plenty powerful enough to take one down on her own. She probably skinned it herself, too.

And this thing, the Book of Plagues, it wasn't happy. It thrashed on the marble, as close to thrashing as an animated magical object could manage, its leather warping and stretching as it struggled unsuccessfully to work its way off the counter. To go where, exactly?

"Relax, little buddy," I said. "You'd just fall right smack on the floor. You're better off waiting for me to extract you."

The book rustled its pages in defiance. Best not to make it angry, I decided. You never knew with these artifacts. Some, I'd been told, could be booby trapped, enchanted with failsafes by their crazy sorcerous owners. A rare few, the really sentient ones, could even cast spells on their own.

I pulled out a third phial, this one filled with a dull purple dust. I know, lots of phials, and a hell of a lot of dust, but it certainly beat hauling around bags of gadgetry everywhere I went. This way Hounds could travel light. It made infiltration easier, and much safer, too. This bottle contained a recent concoction by one of the Lorica's alchemists – Herald himself, actually – and I was told that it'd be perfect for neutralizing, shall we say, more belligerent targets.

The stuff was designed for use on living things, but the way the book was writhing all over the counter I figured it might have a shot of working. I sprinkled some of it across the pages, wincing and holding my breath as the rustling blew some of it upward in a puff of lavender dust.

Still, that seemed to do the trick. Within seconds the grimoire stopped struggling and fluttering as it settled into a quiet, temporary sleep, or whatever semblance of sleep an animated book of shadows was capable of.

And with work out of the way I could take my sweet time, have a little snack. I needed the nutrients to keep growing, or at least that was my excuse. But maybe I'd stopped growing. Pushing six feet at twenty-four, so maybe that was tall enough, but I got hungry when I worked sometimes. Never enough to make myself a sandwich in a stranger's kitchen, but if they had some food sitting out, hey, I wouldn't say no.

Incidentally, there was a bowl of fruit on the counter, and a little tray of chocolate truffles, each wrapped in foil. I helped myself to one – okay, three awfully juicy red grapes, and popped a truffle in my pocket. They wouldn't miss just the one. No big deal, right? Just a couple of treats, nothing serious, or maybe I just thought that way since I had never been averse to a bit of casual thievery.

It started when I was younger, when I learned how to sneak myself a few extra helpings of chicken nuggets at the dinner table while quietly discarding my brussels sprouts. Somehow that transitioned into palming and pocketing trading cards when I was pretending to just check another kid's collection out at school. At most it turned into nicking a drink, hey, maybe a pack of smokes from a convenience store. The smoking never stuck, but the itchy fingers were there to stay.

Which, I suppose, made me ideal for my current occupation. Still I tried not to swipe anything truly valuable from a scene. The worst was a bottle of beer, which got me into real trouble with my supervisor, who said that it was tantamount to drinking on the job, but come on. A guy could get thirsty. And it was one bottle. That was hardly theft. I mean, I got paid enough.

The Eyes got paid better, though. The Hands,

more so. You didn't get much for being just a Hound, which was all kinds of weird since we did lots of field work. Maybe I just got less because I was new. But yeah, Hound work could get so dangerous, too. Sometimes that danger was a dog. Sometimes, if the homeowner was a little crazier, it was a loaded crossbow. But work was work. Just another day on the job. Sniff something out, fetch it.

Speaking of sniffing, that was when it hit me. After the sweetness of the grapes had faded, I caught a whiff of something different in the air. This sharp scent, like metal, and underneath that, something sickly sweet. In retrospect, I should have sensed it earlier, this metallic tang. I figured that it might have been something the Pruitts had left out in the kitchen, but the reality was far worse. Grislier.

I stepped past the kitchen counter, and there they were. Bodies, sprawled on the floor. Two of them, one male, one female, each haloed in mingled pools of blood that still burned angry and red in the gloom. Symbols were daubed on the floor around them, forming a ring in what I could only guess was a kind of ritual circle.

My heart raced, and the inside of my throat went sour. What the hell had happened here? I only knew the Pruitts from studying their dossier, some preliminary web searches, and watching the videos the Lorica had linked for me, but seeing them splayed out like that, with their insides out on the kitchen floor for all to see? That was the kind of intimacy I didn't need. Somehow all the research I'd conducted didn't feel at all like an invasion of privacy, up until the point where I got to see for myself how much blood a person really kept inside them, or how much intestine there really was in the human body.

The near-perfect hole blown straight through Jenna Pruitt's stomach didn't leave much to the imagination. Neither did the matching hole that went right through Hank Pruitt's chest. His heart must have been in there somewhere, strewn amid the gore, one of the pulpier masses on the kitchen tile. It looked like someone had shoved a telephone pole straight through their bodies.

I gagged, and I fought back the urge to retch right there. This wasn't part of the job. I'd never seen dead bodies before. And that smell of rot? I didn't know enough to gauge how long their corpses had been there, but I did know that they couldn't have been dead long enough to start smelling that way.

No, that stench came from the third corpse. The one that had a man's body, but the unmistakeable dead red eyes, whiskered muzzle, and matted fur of a rodent. It was half man, and half giant rat.

Yeah. Just another day on the job.

Chapter 2

"It's a god."

No mistake. That was what one of the guys said, one of the team the Lorica had rushed over to the hillside house the moment I reported the corpses. And no joke, the very moment. The Lorica didn't kid around with efficiency, and it put its best teleporters on the job.

But we're burying the lede. A god. The thing-man-creature with a rat's head was a plague god from the Egyptian pantheon, originally from the Canaanites. Resheph. That was his name.

The first surprise there, of course, was that it was possible to kill gods. The second was the fact that gods existed at all. I had a lot of questions for Thea, but that would have to wait until I got back to HQ. Until then I had to fake enough to pretend that I knew what was going on at all.

Close to twenty men and women had blinked into existence mere minutes after I called in the dilemma. The Lorica's Wings – mages who specialized in teleportation and transportation magic – worked fast.

Then an hour slid by and the hillside house turned into the very picture of a regular crime scene, only – not at all. They were working double duty, collecting evidence, first of all, but also scrubbing the scene of any signs that might point to the crime being anything but achievable in the realm of humanity.

It's not like magic was common knowledge in Valero, or the rest of California, the US, the world, for that matter. We still took pains to keep the wool pulled over the eyes of the everyday joe, the regular folk. The normals.

A small team worked on cleaning up and removing Resheph's remains, because an oversized half human, half rodent was precisely the sort of thing we couldn't have the normals finding in the late Pruitts' household. A woman waved her hands and muttered over the Book of Plagues which had woken up and was angrier than ever, pages ruffling at an aggravated pace. I was pretty sure I could hear the thing growling from where I stood.

And where I stood was the very fringes of the scene. As a Hound, I was good at finding things, seeking stuff out for the Lorica. The rest of the work was best handled by specialists, the way things worked in the normal world. Get the right person for the job. Which is why I found myself wondering why the hell Bastion was even there to begin with.

"Heard you almost threw up," he said, nudging me with one elbow. I grunted in annoyance.

I couldn't stand the guy, with his fringe of impossibly perfect blond hair, eyes that seemed intent on reminding me how much better he was, and a smile designed to charm those he desired and infuriate just about everyone else.

Sebastion Brandt, known to a precious few as Seb, but to most everyone else as Bastion, was one of the Lorica's most talented and most trusted Hands. Everything about his behavior and body language seemed designed specifically to remind everyone that he was at the top of the heap. I mean, I'm a little cocky, I'll admit, but you've never met Bastion.

"Never seen a dead body, huh?" From someone else, that could have been phrased as a genuine, sympathetic question. Out of the sneering grin on Bastion's lips, it was nothing less than a taunt. I just shook my head, eyes focused on everything but his face.

"Oh, leave him alone, Bastion." The voice came from behind me, and I'm not embarrassed to admit that the mere sound of it made Bastion's presence – no, his very existence just that little bit more bearable.

"He's a newbie," the voice continued.

The strong but gentle fingers attached to said voice rubbed me by the shoulder, and I confess, maybe I warmed a little at the gesture. It wasn't like Prudence Leung to be very touchy, and I didn't exactly have a whole lot of friends at the Lorica, so I took every morsel of kindness I could get. She patted me on the shoulder, then stepped up beside me, arms folded, lips curved in an empathetic smile.

"You spoil him too much," Bastion said, eyes darkening.

"No she doesn't," I said.

Prudence chuckled, her eyes glittering as she did, her teeth sparkling. Okay, so maybe they didn't, but she was the kind of pretty that was so disarming that it made you feel like you were watching a shampoo commercial, the kind that made you forget you were standing just feet away from some mangled corpses and several liters of blood.

She ran a hand through her hair, which stopped just short of her shoulder. I was drawn to her fingers, because they were lovely, sure, but also because Prudence was probably the most literal version of a Hand there was.

Like I said, everyone at the Lorica was especially good at something, and that something could get extremely specific. One lady at the scene was using her talent to make the plague-god's body disappear. Whether she was only making it invisible or actually disintegrating the corpse into its basest components, I couldn't really tell.

Bastion could move things without touching them, like telekinesis, which made him crazy useful for all sorts of purposes, but especially combat. As much as I loathed the guy, you haven't lived until you've seen a car being tossed through the air.

Prudence was a skilled martial artist, but that wasn't her gift. I wasn't sure which came first, but her magic complimented the way she fought, because she could concentrate blasts of energy into her strikes. There's nothing quite like watching your coworker punch a hole right through concrete. It's terrifying, and for reasons I can't explain, kind of sexy.

"You're too nice to him. He needs toughening up. Gets bratty because he knows he's mommy's special boy." Bastion flicked his finger at my pendant, the opal dangling from the leather thong at my neck. "A Hound. He's a good little doggie, isn't he? Thea's got him on a leash."

"Quit it," I growled. Bastion was enough of a jerk without all this intrusion into my personal space, and all those damn jokes about how I was my boss's lackey. It wasn't my fault that she trusted me and liked me because I was good at my job. Thea was a good boss, so I tried to be a good worker.

Prudence frowned. "Honestly, Bastion. There's

a line between teasing and outright bullying. Don't call him a dog."

"Oh come on, Prue." Bastion threw his hands up. "He's a Hound. That's his actual job title. You know what? Forget it." He stalked away in a huff, stomping in the direction of the Book of Plagues.

"You'll get used to him."

I sighed. "I've been with you guys nearly a month now. How much longer?"

Prudence just laughed.

"Why is he even here anyway?"

She pointed at the grimoire. Bastion had his hands above it, and the book had stopped its writhing once more. "Suppression is a polite way to put it. Who knows what that book can do?"

I thought back to how I had attempted to taunt the grimoire earlier, and chuckled nervously. "Yeah. Who knows?" I cleared my throat. "How about you?"

"Oh, just supervising. Plus it's good to have a surplus of Hands around anyway, in case something goes down." She bent in closer. "You never know. The killer might still be hanging around."

"I wonder how this even happened to begin with. Who would want to kill a god?"

"Your guess is as good as mine."

"I have way more questions than that, actually. I didn't even know gods existed, to start."

Prudence's lips went tight as she considered her response. "We try to ease new recruits in slowly. It's crazy enough for the newly awakened to discover they can wield magic, or that there's an entire arcane underground separate from reality."

The Veil, they called it, the masquerade us mages were bound to uphold, just to make sure that the world didn't erupt into havoc when they realized that people walking among them could vanish into thin air, call lightning out of the sky, or bend time itself.

"But gods? Really?"

"There's a lot more to it than that. I think it's best if we let Thea guide you through it. But take some friendly advice. You didn't hear it from me, but I'm pretty sure the Black Hand is involved in this."

I blinked. "I'm sorry. The Black Hand?"

Prudence bent closer, her voice dropping. "The Eyes have been at work, and they've picked out that it's some kind of organization. A cult, very likely, that likes to play with the kind of dark magic they really shouldn't have access to. Things like that book you had to retrieve. And murdering a god? Sounds like it's right up their alley."

My blood went cold. A cult? "Prudence. You don't mean to say – this Black Hand. Do you think they were the same people who – you know, did a number on me?" My hand reached reflexively for the scar on my chest, just above my heart.

"It's possible. The Lorica has reason to suspect

that it might well be the same people responsible." She glanced around, then touched me on the back of my hand. "I shouldn't say more. Thea will fill you in the next time you speak, I'm sure of it."

The Black Hand. It had only been weeks since my murder, since the entire incident that set my life down the path that took me to the Lorica. I'd done what I could to shove that all out of my head, but the trauma lingered. Dying wasn't fun. But at least we had a lead, a name for that cabal of strange men in their black robes and their bronze masks. At least I was a step closer to justice. My scar throbbed, and my hand clenched.

I watched on as the Lorica team swept the premises. The house was so much warmer now that it was full of bodies in motion, sweatier, even, as my colleagues went about their business. A couple of Wings were talking about what they had planned for the weekend. Closer to the kitchen, two women spoke in a low murmur as they gesticulated over the Pruitt corpses, preparing their mystical energies for the task ahead.

The women – Hands, both of them, clerics with very specific and very important talents – bent over the Pruitts, each of them picking one of the couple and placing their hands in the air, just inches above their gruesome wounds.

Ever mixed up some mac and cheese from the box, or maybe some carbonara, right when you stirred it up with the raw eggs? That was the sound the corpses made when their flesh began to knit itself right before our eyes, squishing and squelching as muscle and fat and skin spontaneously regenerated to narrow the gaping holes in their bodies.

A faint, yellowish light permeated the space between the women's hands and the Pruitts' bodies, a manifestation of their magic, the way that Prudence's fists glowed a vibrant blue when she punched things into oblivion. The Hands kept working, closing the wounds tightly enough so that they only resembled knife stabs and not – well, who knows what was even used to kill them in the first place? A cannonball?

"Still amazes me, what people can do," Prudence muttered.

"Hmm? You mean how they're closing the wounds, or are you talking about whoever murdered the Pruitts?"

"Both, probably." Prudence shook her head. "All this work the team is putting into making it look like a murder. You know the sad reality of it? This happens in the real world all the time anyway, normals killing each other left and right. The news will go nuts for this, but that'll fade. Nobody's going to miss a couple of dead bodies."

"Hey, we're doing the best we can, too." I patted her on the shoulder. "The normals have their police and their people to help them with this stuff. We're just making sure they don't have any reason to panic."

And normally, they didn't, but a spell book that could be used to create magical pestilence, and two normals dead? Not to mention a slain god. Something was definitely up. I wanted to reassure Prudence, but this was all making me a little nervous, too.

Like Thea always said, the Lorica's purpose was damage control, to stop absolute chaos from happening. However bad it was out in the regular world, it could always go worse if some psycho, or hell, just someone who had no idea what they were doing got their hands on a deadly artifact. The Book of Plagues, for example.

Sure, medical technology has made it so that the plague is total peanuts to cure, but bungle an incantation, or throw in the wrong reagents? Amateur, unpracticed magic could easily create hellish epidemics. That was exactly the kind of scale things could fuck up on when spells went sideways: mass destruction, genocide, possibly even extinction. Whoever this Black Hand was probably had designs on setting off a new form of the plague, bioterrorism at its very worst.

Lights flashed, cameras flickering as the Lorica team worked to capture the scene. Everyone in that house was a magic user, sure, but magic still couldn't beat the sheer convenience of recording images with a DSLR, or a good old smart phone. Technology came into play all the time at the Lorica, especially when it involved communication, though, as the opal at my throat began to warm gently, I recalled that there were a few exceptions.

And what perfect timing for Bastion to amble up to us again, his hands folded behind his head, eyebrow cocked and lips crooked like he couldn't have been more bored. Prudence tapped her foot and sucked on her teeth.

"Really, Brandt? You done already?"

Bastion shrugged. "Easy peasy. The book put up a fight, but it'll be safe enough to transport back to HQ."

He jerked his head in my direction and snaked out one hand to flick at my pendant. And like that wasn't enough, he hooked a finger under the leather cord, then tugged.

"Your rock is glowing again. Mommy's calling. Shouldn't you pick up?"

"Step off," I muttered, swatting at his hand hard enough that it made a loud smack.

Bastion stepped back and sneered. "Watch yourself there, maverick, or you'll find out what happens to bad little puppies."

Prudence grabbed him by the wrist. "Jesus, Bastion, you started it. Just leave the kid alone. Honestly." She shoved him back, and sure, maybe Bastion had several inches on her, and a couple dozen pounds of muscle to boot, but Prudence had this way of making people stop and pay attention to what she was saying. It might have to do with how she could crush skulls into powder with her bare hands.

"You really should pick up," she said, nodding at my necklace.

"Yeah. Sorry. Gotta take this."

I went into a corner, returning Bastion's last dirty glance with one of my own, then touched a finger to my pendant. That was how Thea taught me to establish the connection. The gem was enchanted to enable an intently private form of communication between us. Telepathy, essentially.

Maybe Thea was especially mistrustful of cellphone technology, or maybe she just didn't want anyone snooping. I just found it amusing how it felt almost exactly like picking up a phone anyway. The opal was how I reported the Pruitt situation to the Lorica – well, to Thea – in the first place.

I cleared my throat, then felt silly for doing so since we only ever spoke with our thoughts. "Thea," I said, or thought. Bear with me. "What's up?"

It wasn't just words that got channeled when these conversations happened, and sometimes I could get glimmers of emotion, or flashes of imagery too. Something reddish pulsed in my mind's eye, like a kind of concern, or a quiet panic. Maybe it was just our dynamic, but I knew what Thea was going to say before she even transmitted it.

"We need to talk."

Chapter 3

Bastion zipped up his leather jacket, then paused as he held his motorcycle helmet just above his head with all the pomp and ceremony of a king at his own coronation.

"You can make your own way back, can't you?" he said, barely containing his snigger. "I only have the one helmet. It'd be super illegal, not to mention irresponsible, to have you ride with me."

"I'll be fine," I said, doing my best to overlook his false concern. I didn't want to be caught dead riding pillion on Bastion's bike, because first of all, being in the same room with him was already too close for comfort, and second, that thing was a certified death trap. I was willing to take a couple of risks at work, but I had no intention of meeting my second death in a flaming motorcycle accident.

Bastion shrugged, slipped on his helmet, then blew me a mocking kiss. Even through the tint of glass I could sense his eyes laughing at me. Then he revved the engine a couple of times – loud and hard, like the jerk he was – and took off on his motorcycle, looking for all the world like a massive asshole.

The cleanup had taken so much time and detail that the sun was already up. There were still a couple of people in the Pruitt house working on concealing the last of the supernatural evidence, but the rest of us were clear to head out. I was so looking forward to reporting to Thea, then possibly begging off for the rest of the morning to get some shuteye. I asked Prudence if she wanted to head back to the Lorica together.

"Sorry, champ. I'm actually off to another assignment." She tapped at her cellphone, lips pursed as she called for a car. "And HQ isn't on the way. You going to be fine?"

"Yeah. Sure. Don't worry about it."

"You should call a car, too. Put it on the Lorica's dime."

I shrugged. "I might just walk it. I could use the exercise." I smiled and waved, stuffing my hands into my jacket pockets as I turned to go. "See you around."

Prudence waved back, then turned her attention back to her phone. I could use the exercise? What the hell was I saying? I was exhausted. I'd been up the whole night, and I was still tired from breaking into the Pruitts', not to mention the fact that I hadn't eaten in hours.

I guess I didn't want to hang around and wait for her car to show up, or for mine to come when I got around to requesting one. I mean I was generally great with people, but something about Prudence intimidated me a little. She was only a bit older than me, probably in her late twenties, but she had her shit together, whereas I had only just started my shit-togethering journey.

I had the Lorica to thank for that. Hell, I had the Lorica to thank for a lot of things, but especially how I had a better understanding of what it was that made me so different from any other idiot kid on the street. It was Thea who explained that we discovered the arcane within us at different paces, and through different means. Mine just happened to be triggered by extreme stress.

Who could say if there were plenty of triggers that could be considered more dire than a knife through the heart, but I suppose that counted as extreme enough. It was the Lorica that took me in after that whole bloody incident, and it was the closest thing to stable employment as I'd ever gotten. The biggest perk, of course, was getting to learn more about what I could do – what I am – and how I could use that to make the world a little less crappier in general.

My stomach grumbled again. That was right. I still had the truffle I'd appropriated from the Pruitts' kitchen. I pried it out of my pockets, fumbling to unwrap it, maybe a little too excited to pop it in my mouth. Give me a break, okay, that sandwich I had for dinner clearly didn't last. I let the truffle sit in my cheek, the cocoa powder spreading across my tongue, dark chocolate slowly melting.

I wondered how many of these Hank Pruitt liked to eat in a day. I wondered if he had any inkling last night that he didn't have much time left to enjoy more truffles, or much of anything else. I shook my head and sighed. It was like Thea and the Scions always tried to impress upon us at the Lorica. We did our jobs to make sure people like the Pruitts didn't end up the way they did.

Protection was our purpose, and that was what the word Lorica actually meant: armor. Thea had told me that the day she recruited me, and I looked it up after, just to be sure. It was body armor, specifically, the kind that the ancient Romans wore as breastplates. So the Lorica was the torso, and the rest of us functioned in concert as its parts, the Hands, the Wings, the Eyes, and so on, working together to guard both the regular world and the arcane underground from the very worst that magic could do. But I couldn't help thinking that we had stumbled. We had three corpses on our hands, after all.

Still, we couldn't very well save everyone, and

we were doing everything we could to mop up in the aftermath. I sighed, my breath tumbling out in a puff of fog. Valero could get pretty chilly in the morning, and I was lucky at least that it wasn't so windy out in the streets that particular day. I eyed the shadows cast by the buildings in the neighborhood, so sorely tempted to step into them and make my commute that much shorter, but that would have been about as subtle as taking off my pants and screaming "Look I'm a wizard" while streaking down the boulevard. Sure, I was entering a commercial district, and not a lot of people were up and about just yet, but it was the type of thing that Thea would have been quick to label as showboating. The Lorica didn't like that.

They didn't like it when their people got too flashy, or took dumb risks, especially when the risk wasn't just exposure. I was told that I could make greater leaps, bigger steps once I had a better handle on shadowstepping, but I was supposed to stick to line of sight for now. I'd heard way too many horror stories about Lorica Wings and teleporters who bit off more than they could chew and ended up shifting themselves into unfamiliar spaces – like the middle of the ocean, for example.

I very briefly reconsidered calling a car, but after finding myself a little bit out of breath from having walked just two miserable blocks, decided that I probably did need the exercise after all. Not so far now anyway, I told myself. I could just make out HQ from where I was walking, this squat, ugly building just on the edge of Central Square. It made me chuckle every time I saw HQ from this vantage, how it looked like a lumpy sack of potatoes next to the glamor of so many glitzy office buildings, hotels, and restaurants.

I pushed the white plastic button on the facade of the little structure the Lorica called home. It had a concrete exterior, the kind that looked like it was studded with pebbles so that it was all knobbly, making it seem almost vintage, nostalgic. It made the building just shy of hip enough to fit in with the heart of Valero, despite being so bland and uninteresting. The best word to use to describe HQ was nondescript, just the way the Lorica liked it. In modern parlance, it was very "Meh."

A static-muffled voice sounded out through the ancient speaker, its yellowed plastic in stark contrast to the faux dark stone finish of the facade. "Password," the voice asked.

I looked around to make sure no one was in earshot, recalled it was a Tuesday, then bent in closer and whispered. "Manticore." A different word for every day of the week, and sometimes the sequence changed, which wasn't much of a pain when admin remembered to email us a fresh batch of codes.

The speaker crackled back with something vague and noncommittal, and a low click from the door told me that it was safe to enter. That was crucial, see. The Scions liked to keep a contingency of protection spells active, just in case. They were more like traps, really, and the whole point of buzzing in was to make sure nobody accidentally walked through and took several fireballs straight to the face.

A gust of warm air welcomed me as the door swung inward, a nice change from the cold of the early Valero morning. The warmth wasn't from an internal heating system, either, but from one of several magic-fed fires kept burning throughout the building, whether from braziers or fireplaces. No wood or coal, so no smoke. Why resort to magical flames, you ask? Who knew. The Scions had their own way of doing things.

That, and maybe the fact that the fire went with the decor, and the reality that everyone who worked at the Lorica was, in some shape of form, a real life frigging wizard. The inside of the Lorica was honest to goodness like the interior of some enormous library, looking like it had been hewn out of only the most expensive lacquered wood, the floors carpeted in massive, sumptuous rugs, all the light coming from eldritch flames flickering in polished brass candelabras, or smokeless fireplaces, or the aforementioned braziers positioned in every corner.

Did I mention that the place was huge? Because that's important. You could see all the action from the mezzanine, but for the most part every department could be found on one of only two floors. From the outside, HQ looked like it could be about the size and importance of a local post office. The interior, however, seemed to stretch on for at least a mile along both axes. I didn't know how the geometry of it all worked out, but for whatever the Lorica paid in terms of property tax, I'd say that it was pretty damn worth it.

And the style – the utter, heartbreaking style of the place was something else. It was a magical office for magical people, after all, so it wasn't uncommon to see paper planes sailing through corridors, or books flapping their pages like birds. Sure, it was just as easy to fire off an email or get a courier to do all that, but this was the Lorica we were talking about.

From where I stood, a sleek, spiny dragon made out of sheaves of documents roared and flew from one end of the library to the other. I guessed that it was heading towards the accounting department. Sure, they had to do tons of paperwork, but they definitely knew how to make it fun.

Further off from the central work area alchemists stirred and scrambled colorful liquids and reagents in bubbling beakers and flasks full of who-knows-what, their laboratory set apart to avoid mishaps, just in case something exploded.

The astrolabes, sextants, and compasses set by the huge, glowing map of the earth that the Eyes used to do their surveillance work made it feel like a proper magician's study, albeit a massive one. It was every fantasy nerd's wet dream, and that's without even mentioning all the cool artifacts and devices they kept in the Gallery.

It was a conundrum, how they fit all that into the building. I had considered that maybe the exterior was just some kind of illusion, versus the possibility that the enormity of HQ's insides meant that it dwelled within its own pocket dimension. Nobody had a straight answer for me, not even folks who had worked there for years, and the Scions probably wanted to keep things that way. It helped keep the Lorica and its secrets secure.

"Heya, Dustin," the girl at reception cooed, peering around from behind her flatscreen monitor. Her cheeks lifted as she smiled in greeting, the beautiful bronze of them going just a bit rosier, or so I liked to believe.

I ran my fingers through my hair, black and a little clingy to my forehead, brushing it out of my face and grinning, because people seemed to like it when I did that. It brought attention to my eyes which, as many women have said, are the best part of my face.

Okay, fine. It was just my mom. Shush.

"Hey yourself, Romira," I said, giving her my best smile.

She cocked her shoulder, black hair spilling in waves over her back, her lips just friendly enough, but never too friendly. She had all the trappings of a sweetheart, with a pretty smile and laughing eyes, which made her seem totally harmless. The keyword was seem. That was probably why the Scions liked to keep her up front.

Romira just looked like a nice young woman who worked in reception, but she was supposedly one of our most powerful Hands, the literal beast that guarded the gates. She also occasionally put in work as an Eye, which was the first I'd heard of anyone at the Lorica doing double duty. Her specialties were probably what made her so ideal for manning the front desk.

Anyone who miraculously made it past the traps up front had to contend with Romira. I'd never seen exactly what it was she could do, but office gossip told me that the last poor soul who thought they could barge their way through ended up as a greasy black smear on the floor, which they kept covered up with a rug in the center of the room. I tried to stay on her good side, which, frankly, wasn't that hard considering how she was always nice to me anyway. And I mean really nice.

She leaned her chin into her hand, drumming her fingers on her desk and putting on a piteous expression. "Aww. Rough night, Dust? You look exhausted."

"Totally destroyed," I said, shrugging. "But you know how it is, gotta come to work anyway.

The boss wants to see me."

Romira cocked her head, her smile spreading wider. "Lots of people want to see you, Dust."

"I. Uh." I chuckled nervously, scratched at the back of my neck, and cleared my throat. "Gotta go." Like I said, I could be good with people, but only to a point. Being charming was easy until someone tried to be charming right back, and Romira played this game like a grandmaster.

Her eyes twinkled a kind of red as she laughed, her teeth sharp and glinting. "Come back here," she teased. "I'm not done with you."

I half-stopped and half-stumbled away from her desk, watching as she muttered and wove her fingers over the reception area, drawing an intricate web out of pale fire. She ended the spell with a snap, and the pattern vanished.

"Take over for me, Mary," she said.

I knew about Mary by then. That was the name Romira gave to the elemental construct she sometimes used to staff the reception desk when she had to use the ladies', or, as in this case, when she felt the need to taunt me a little bit more. Mary manifested out of thin air, a wispy silhouette of a woman made out of orange fire. The construct put on Romira's headset, then answered a call in a voice I could best describe as sultry, and a little smokey.

"Honestly jealous that you can do that, you know."

Romira smirked. "We all learn at our own

pace, Dust. You've been here what, a few weeks now? Took me ages to master how to summon Mary, much less get her to pick up a phone. Also to stop her from setting everything on fire."

Mary penciled something into a legal pad, then gave us a thumbs up.

"Still can't manifest her for too long, though, I need more practice. But I'm just famished. Gotta take a break. Walk with me to the pantry?"

She didn't have to ask twice. My stomach grumbled, and I resisted the urge to swipe one of the candies she kept in a bowl on her desk. I'd never seen her eat one, and probably for good reason.

I'd once noticed that the candy bowl was almost empty, only to watch as the leftover pieces just sort of started – wriggling. Writhing against each other, like they were trying to reproduce. The bowl was full again the next morning. When I say I watch what I put inside my body, it's not about me trying my best to be a good Californian. There really were certain things that I would rather not let slip past my mouth, and several of them lived inside the Lorica.

But the coffee at HQ was pretty good, which was why I happily followed Romira to the break room. She poured us a couple of cups from a device that looked far more like an alchemical apparatus than a coffee press.

They had some muffins set out as well, those ridiculous triple chocolates ones that I liked so much. Romira snatched one for herself, balancing it on her coffee cup, then threw me a wink before trotting off back to her station. That left me alone in the break room, which was just fine by me since it gave me the privacy I needed to shove the muffin straight down my gullet.

I ambled off towards the Gallery, the hub of shelves and display cases the Lorica used to store the artifacts us Hounds retrieved for them. This was where two of my closer friends at HQ tended to hang out. I looked around for Herald, a Gallery archivist who also doubled as one of the Lorica's best alchemists, and found him wrestling with the Book of Plagues.

Wrestling might not have been the right word for it. Black-haired, bespectacled, and dressed like the snappiest librarian I'd ever seen, Herald Igarashi had his hands thrust out against the book, muttering to himself as violet skeins of light surged from his fingers. The Book of Plagues flapped and struggled in defiance.

I rushed forward, ready to assist when the book jerkily leapt up from Herald's desk to snap at his fingers. Fury twisted his features, and before I could bother to help, Herald balled his hand into a fist and punched the book square in its leather-bound cover. The book screeched, then fell to the desk, its pages fluttering limply.

"Stay down, damn it." Herald adjusted his tie, then nudged his glasses up the bridge of his nose.

"That's a mean left hook. Uh. Need help?"

"Can't talk," Herald muttered, wiping a hand against his forehead. "Gotta get this son of a bitch in cold storage before it starts fighting back again."

"That sleeping dust you gave me worked wonders before."

"Oh?" Herald's eyes lit up, to show that he found my suggestion helpful, or perhaps because he considered it a compliment. He did create the powder after all. He lunged across his workspace, reaching for a phial of the purple dust, then promptly dumped it all over the grimoire. The book's pages fluttered, then went limp.

"Thanks for the tip," he said, sighing with some relief. "Gonna go grab a case to put this in. Bulletproof one, just to be safe. I'll probably chain it up, too." He cracked his knuckles, then favored me with a small grin. "Talk later?"

I gave him a salute as he walked off into the archives to hunt for supplies. Herald's work was pretty serious, making sure the artifacts stayed put exactly where they were, especially the ones that, in the wrong hands, could cause widespread disaster.

Eyeing the Book of Plagues and noting that it was pretty much unconscious, I headed over to another section of the Gallery, to a glass display case where a sword lay across a velvet cushion. The blade and scabbard were cast from tarnished bronze, aged to a murky green with verdigris. Deep red garnets decorated its hilt, jewels that seemed duller, dimmer than the last time I'd visited.

"Vanitas," I said. "Hey. You in there?"

The sword said nothing. Now, I'm going to sound totally crazy, but this was that other friend I was talking about. Some weeks back I'd been tasked to retrieve this very artifact, what I'd been informed was basically a magic sword. Nobody told me it could talk, or fly of its own accord, or even fight, which was how Vanitas and I became friends. I was in the Meathook, a really rough part of Valero, and some thugs were bothering me. He sprang to life, beat them up, then cut off one of their hands. It was this whole thing, and it was so, so awesome.

But Vanitas had gone silent the day I brought him back to the Gallery. Herald tried to tell me that it must have been my imagination, that the sword's enchantment might have been to cast that very illusion and convince me it could talk, and fly, and fight. But I swear I'm not insane. I could remember Vanitas's voice so clearly, yet all he'd done for weeks was sit perfectly still on his cushion. I tapped at the glass.

"Vanitas. Yo. It's me, Dustin."

Still no response. I sighed and turned away, just in time for Herald to come back with a trolley loaded with a fresh glass case and some incredibly sturdy-looking chains. Enchanted, of course, because nobody wanted something as aggressive and vile as the Book of Plagues breaking its way out and wreaking havoc in the Gallery.

It took some heavy lifting, but together we managed to strap the book down and negotiate it into its new home. Prison, more like. I thought of Vanitas again, wondering whether that was why he had gone silent.

"Herald. These cases, are they enchanted or something? I mean, in some way to nullify an artifact's power?"

He cocked an eyebrow and shook his head. "Never. The point of the Gallery is to keep these relics safe, not to destroy or neuter them completely. The chains are there to restrain the tougher bastards." He gave the book's display case a half-hearted kick. "But no. The glass is mostly protective."

"Okay," I said, trying not to show my disappointment. "Thanks for explaining."

There had to be another reason Vanitas was lying dormant. But if Herald had no answers, then what chance did I really stand of solving the mystery of the sword's silence myself?

I left Herald to his work then. It was cool to have a few friends at the Lorica, whether it was him, or Romira, or Prudence. Everyone was happy to help each other out, I'd noticed, and I was always glad to extend a hand whether or not somebody asked. Unless, of course, that person happened to be Bastion.

Who, incidentally, I hadn't seen since getting

to HQ, which was weird considering he probably beat me there on his speeding death bullet of a motorcycle, but that was just as well. I turned a corner as I grudgingly made my way to Thea's office, dreading what it was that she wanted to talk about, when I came face to face with exactly the person I was trying to avoid.

"Beat you to it," Bastion said. "Weren't you supposed to be here sooner?" He jerked a thumb over his shoulder. "She wanted to see you, like, yesterday."

"I get it, Bastion. I just had to check on the grimoire first."

He cocked an eyebrow. "Whatever for? I made sure it was fine, and it's fine." The corner of his mouth lifted, how it always did when he got into one of his taunting moods. "Oh. Of course. You just wanted a chance to check in on your imaginary friend, didn't you?"

I hid my cough by forcing down another swig of my coffee. "I don't know what you mean." I hated it when Bastion successfully zeroed in on my tender little weak spots, and that was exactly what he had done.

"It's just a busted old sword, Dusty." Man, I especially hated it when he called me Dusty. Bastion's grin grew wider, enough that I could see both rows of his irritatingly perfect teeth. "I know you think that the two of you went on a little adventure, but honestly. It was just your imagination." He winked, and I fought to keep a straight face as my insides burned.

Bastion could be such an asshole. I opened my mouth to say so when, further down the corridor, someone's head poked around the corner. I went rigid. The Lorica stuck to its own rules and rituals, sure, but at the end of the day, it was still an organization, as close to a corporation as the magical world could get. There was no room in a professional setting for on-the-job altercations, especially not when Thea was watching.

She cleared her throat, and even from that distance Bastion knew to be on his best behavior as well. His posture went ramrod straight, and he leaned against the nearest wall in a quick attempt to look nonchalant, suddenly so interested in his fingernails. Thea cocked her head, her short, insanely stylish crop of hair staying put as she did, then quirked her lips in the direction of her office.

"About time, Dustin," she said. "Come on. I need you in my office. Now."

Chapter 4

Quiet. That was the first word that came to mind each time I went into Thea's office. The other was immaculate. Kind of hard to avoid that association since the entire room – generally, even Thea's clothing – would be stark white.

I hadn't stepped into many executive offices around HQ, but I'd come to understand that they were allowed to decorate as they pleased, their spaces becoming reflections of their inner selves. Kind of gave new meaning to interior decorating considering how Thea's office looked absolutely nothing like the corridors outside. There weren't any fires in there either, just little suspended globes of what looked like sunlight. Also, everything smelled of sandalwood.

I drained my coffee as fast as I could, gulping

it down in three mouthfuls, because when your boss asks you to take a seat on the white leather chair perched on the white throw rug right across from her fully translucent plexiglass desk, you do everything in your power to avoid spilling things. Coffee, blood, hell, any speck of color would be out of place there. Thea kept things so tidy and pristine that her workspace was essentially what an archangel's office might look like.

That was the sort of presence and authority she commanded, too. She folded her hands together on her desk, watching me closely, and smiling, but for all the warmth in her lips, all I could see was a lioness. Her eyes studied me with the intense, almost uncomfortable keenness of a predator, and her coif of neat, closely-cropped blonde hair could serve as either a mane, or a halo. Throw all that into a stylish ivory pantsuit and a collection of enchanted opalescent jewelry and you'd have a decent picture of the woman I worked for, this creature that I at once admired and, I hoped, not-so-obviously feared.

"So," she said. "Things are not great."

I nodded. "Kind of an understatement."

"Which is why we need to shore up our defenses, even on a personal level." She placed her hands flat on the table, then leaned forward. "Time for you to learn about communing with the entities."

"Entities?" The hair at my nape bristled. "You mean gods?"

She pursed her lips, her gaze thoughtful. "I suppose that works, but not all entities are gods. It's a blanket name we use for all sorts of powerful beings that coexist with us."

"Gotta admit, I didn't even know they existed before last night."

"In retrospect, I should have briefed you about them earlier. I just never thought it would come up so soon in your time with the Lorica. But consider it part of your training." She steepled her hands together, resting her chin on the points of her fingers.

"Many of the creatures and deities you've read about in myth, even the monsters and demons and spirits, a lot of their stories persist for a reason. Some of them have always just been around. Others were manifested into being, because even the nonmagical, normal human mind has a funny way of being able to create things out of thin air if it believes strongly enough."

"And they just exist?" I moved my hand in a circle. "Like, just around us."

"In a manner of speaking, yes. And speaking of speaking, it's time you learned to communicate with them. Commune, even. The entities are useful for a lot of things, mainly gathering information, but sometimes one might like you enough to grant you a boon. A physical gift, maybe, or they might even lend you a bit of their power."

My eyes widened. "I thought you said that sharpening our specialties or learning more magic were the only ways to make real progress."

"Well, that, and making the right friends. Even if those friends are ancient demigods and cacodemons. As in real life, there are shortcuts for everything, and as in real life, sometimes it's not what you know. It's who you know."

Her eyes flitted, and she rested her chin in her hand. "But there are caveats. I wonder if I should tell you." She paused for thought, then cleared her throat. "Well, yes. All right. So you take the deities and supernatural creatures, and broadly, the Lorica classifies them all as entities. And they run the gamut from inconsequential – smaller, less significant spirits – to completely terrifying. We're talking heads of pantheons here, archdemons, the great beasts: the All-Father, the Trimurti, Asmodeus, Leviathan, Tiamat. The very biggest kahunas. But theoretically, the most powerful beings of all surpass the entities. You don't want to get mixed up in all that. There is a class of them that aren't found in mythology. They're stranger, stronger, more vicious, worse than the entities in every way."

I hadn't realized my mouth was hanging open, and I made sure to shut it. Just some time back I hadn't even known that magic existed, and then this? I was starting to understand why Thea kept some of it from me. Learning everything about the Veil all at once would have completely fractured my mind.

"The Eldest," Thea said, her voice a quiet mix of fear and reverence, "are older, greater than all the gods of the earth. And they have no concept, no understanding of humanity. The gods of myth, demons, all the rest, they're clearly rooted in the human experience. Look at the Greek pantheon, especially. They live, they love, they fight, they die. The Eldest are nothing like that. They're primal forces, fundamental to the universe, and their only instinct is to edge ever closer to domination, whether that power comes from breeding madness, or mayhem, or slaughter. The entities cannot possibly compare."

I finally swallowed. "Right," I said hoarsely. "Entities can be good or bad, but the Oldest – "

"The Eldest," Thea corrected. "Yes. They're worse still. And best not to bring it up again. I only wanted you to be aware that they existed. Oh, but another thing. Unrelated."

She leaned forward again, her head lowering towards her desk, like she had something conspiratorial to share. I mirrored her posture, bending in closer. "We probably don't want you gallivanting out on your own for a little while. You found the Pruitt corpses and the god Resheph, after all. Whoever wanted them dead might find out about you."

I twiddled my thumbs. "I like going out on my own."

Thea frowned. "Not going to happen anymore.

Not for a while, at least. Things are getting dangerous out there. Even the higher-ups are talking about this. No one is happy. Least of all the Pruitts, with those holes blown through their bodies." Her features softened, as did her voice. "This is what I meant when we met, Dustin. Remember? Protecting people from their own greed, from power they don't understand. It's why you do what you do. And you're so good at it."

She was right. Hound or no, it didn't make sense for me to work on my own anymore, which made me a little sad, frankly speaking. But sad was better than dead.

"I do question that sometimes, you know. I mean, I'm just a Hound."

"Just a Hound," Thea mimicked. She drew back, her face going hard. "Who told you that? Nonsense. You're just as important to the Lorica as anyone." She reached out, clasping my hand, the gold of her many rings cool against my skin, her opals glowing like little suns. "You're valuable to us, Dustin. To me. You are special. Don't let anyone tell you otherwise."

I didn't return her gaze, but I nodded.

"You're like a son to me, kid."

I didn't know if Thea intended for me to notice, but her eyes swept past the monitor of her computer and landed on a couple of framed photographs on her desk. Pictures of her kids, a boy and a girl, but old ones that were obviously taken some time back. Nothing recent. I never asked about her children, or why she never had new pictures of them. Maybe that was why we understood each other. She had lost part of her own family, the way I'd lost part of mine.

"Don't forget why you're here. We still need to find who did this to you." Her eyes fell on my chest, staring there like she could see through my shirt. The scar over my heart itched just then. I reached for it and scratched. Thea knew everything that happened, anyway. No sense hiding that I still found it difficult to talk about my death.

"Someone mentioned the Black Hand," I said, carefully.

Thea's eyes narrowed. "Office gossip spreads fast, I see. Yes. We have reason to believe that this Black Hand is the same organization behind all of these recent incidents: Resheph's murder, the Pruitts', even yours."

"It doesn't make sense, though. If they had plans to spread some new kind of magical plague, why did they leave the book?"

"Perhaps the Black Hand got what they came for. I think this goes deeper. Resheph was only vulnerable because he stepped outside of his home dimension. That's the only way a god gets killed, and the only reason a god would leave is for something extremely important – say, taking the Book of Plagues away so that no one would ever bother him with a summoning again. The

Pruitts were just dabblers, fools playing at magic. Likely just casualties along the way."

I squinted, trying to unravel the scenario. "So you're saying that the Pruitts summoned Resheph, just to see if they could, and the Black Hand was already waiting to – to what, exactly? Were they after the Pruitts, or the god himself?"

"As I said, the Pruitts are inconsequential. Unfortunate that they died, to be sure, but they were collateral damage. You see, a god's death comes with its own repercussions. It leaves a gap in our reality, and while the world rushes to fill that void, we see and feel the aftereffects. In Resheph's case it could be as awful as an epidemic, or as minor as some restless rodents."

A shuffling sound made its way across the wall just behind Thea's head. She tutted and rolled her eyes.

"Restless rodents it is, then. It'll be chaos for some time. Expect to find lots of overactive rats. Think of it as Resheph's disappearance causing reverberations across his former dominion, his area of power. But more importantly: we need to remain vigilant. The Black Hand may strike again. But who knows when?"

The scratching noises continued, making it seem as if there were at least a dozen of those rats maneuvering between the walls. I shifted uncomfortably, wondering if the Lorica had its own way of dealing with vermin. But the scuffling stopped when someone knocked on Thea's office.

"Come in," Thea said.

I turned my head to follow the door when it swung open, and in stepped Odessa, one of the Lorica's Scions. She favored a more esoteric kind of fashion, keeping to conservative dresses and long, black hair that framed her face with severe bangs, and looked for all the world like a living, breathing doll.

The Scions were the Lorica's elders, high-ranking mages who were more learned or experienced than the rest of us, whether through skill or seniority. It was tough looking at Odessa and thinking the words elder or senior could ever apply considering she looked just shy of eighteen, which wasn't to say anything of her mastery. There was just something off about her, in the depth of her voice, the deliberateness and confidence of her gestures. Her presence was laden with the kind of gravity that came from immense inner storehouses of power and knowledge.

If the water cooler talk was true, she was actually a little over a hundred years old, though how that translated to her appearance none ever dared to ask or even pry. It was the mage's most coveted mystery, after all: the secret to eternal life, or at least, to longevity.

We all had our specialties, granted, but the surest way for a mage to continue growing in power was through studying the Lorica's immense collection of scrolls and grimoires.

According to Thea, that kind of learning and mastery could take years, even decades.

The more time a mage had to study, the more they absorbed into their occult arsenal, and the greater their power. A mage who could wield fire was one thing, but a mage who also knew how to fly, turn invisible, and summon demons on command? That was the stuff of nightmares. I couldn't guess at all the things Odessa knew, all the mysteries that she had unraveled.

Odessa turned from Thea to me, nodding with the curtest of silent greetings. I took that as my cue to leave. I stood bolt upright, gave Thea a small wave, then almost found myself bowing to Odessa. She didn't seem to notice, but Thea's sharp intake of breath told me that she found the little unintentional jerk of my head amusing.

"I'll be in touch, Dustin," she said, keeping her face straight. "Get some sleep for now. You've got the rest of the day off."

Keeping my face stock-still, I sucked in my cheeks, doing my honest best to hide how thrilled I was to have a chance to recover from the events of last night. I was self-conscious enough about disguising my glee without having Odessa in the room. The Scions just made me nervous. Maybe it was how nobody knew for sure what any of them could do, magically speaking. Something about her told me that she had power enough to wipe me off the face of the planet with just a crook of her pinky finger.

I shut the door quietly behind me and glanced at my phone. It was barely past ten. I stretched my arms out as I sauntered off, happy to get some time to myself at last. But not five feet down the corridor I felt my opal pendant warm up again.

Groaning, I glanced down, spotting the faint glow at my neck. What now? I was supposed to have the rest of the day off. I sighed and touched two fingers to the stone. Thea's voice in my head sounded distant, laden with echoes.

"Dustin? Sorry, I can sense you're disappointed, but I promise you can take the day off tomorrow. There's stuff that needs doing. I'll meet you out front once I'm done with Odessa. What are your thoughts on lunch? Chinese? My treat."

"Sure," I thought back, doing my hardest to pretend that I wasn't bummed. "Why not? What's the occasion?"

"Well, I'm hungry, for one," she transmitted. "Also, you'll need to eat up, get some strength back. Today, you're going to meet your very first entity."

Chapter 5

"Eat that up," Thea said, piling more food on my plate. "It's good for you."

She'd been doing that all throughout lunch, transferring slices of meat and delicious hunks of deep-fried this and that with her chopsticks directly onto my ever-growing heap of food.

"You're too skinny," she said through a mouthful of rice, not for the first time since we got there. I grinned sheepishly, a little puzzled by why she was so concerned, but admittedly flattered that she cared.

I liked it when she got all maternal like that. I complied, doing my best with my own chopsticks, popping another dumpling into my mouth. The wrapper burst as I bit into it, releasing a hot gush of soup that the geniuses at the Seven Dragons restaurant had somehow managed to smuggle into the dumpling.

"Xiao long bao," Thea explained earlier, after I had very visibly expressed my elation over this tasty new treat. "Really clever. They chill the broth with gelatin before putting it in the wrapper with the meat. Then when they steam it, it all turns into soup. Delicious." And delicious was right. I'd eaten six of the suckers already.

Although I still had no idea why we were there at all. The Seven Dragons was a lot fancier than the Chinese places I was used to eating at. I mean there were plenty of options for dining around Valero, but nothing quite like this.

The faint music piping through the restaurant switched readily between Asian pop and what Thea generously described as Chinese opera. The interiors themselves were finished in rich silken red, with golden sculptures and accents here and there. And the dining area itself, of course, smelled delicious. But I knew that this wasn't just about a guy and his boss eating out.

I swallowed another dumpling, and another mouthful of rice. "This isn't what I was expecting," I told her.

"How do you mean? I told you, there's way more to Chinese cuisine than egg rolls. Or orange chicken, which isn't even truly Chinese. Did you know that Americans came up with that? Kind of dilutes the experience, if you ask me."

One thing to know about Thea was that she

was chockfull of these informational tidbits, little factoids about whatever it was we were currently experiencing. It was never to show off, that much I knew, but I could never shake the feeling that she sometimes did it in an attempt to disarm me, or to distract from the truth of the matter.

"It's not that," I said, pushing a grain of rice around on my plate. "I mean I knew we were coming out for lunch, but you did mention that other thing." I leaned forward over the table, glancing to either side of me before speaking in a softer voice. "You know. Meeting an entity."

"Ah. That." Thea leaned back and set down her chopsticks. She patted at her lips with a napkin, then smiled. "Would you believe me if I told you that this was all part of it? We're gathering reagents." She raised a hand, beckoning our waitress over.

"Uh. Reagents? From a Chinese restaurant?"

Thea nodded, at me, then at our waitress. She fired off a fluent barrage of phrases in Chinese, the second time she had done it that day. The waitress nodded, grinning, then scuttled off.

I couldn't help myself. "So you speak Chinese?"

There was a quirk in Thea's smile, but there was no trace of condescension when she spoke. "Mandarin, actually. And a little, yes. Mostly enough to order in a Chinese restaurant." She smiled in a way that told me that wasn't true.

I wondered how much else Thea was hiding,

how many other talents this woman had. I couldn't help feeling a little bit smaller considering how badly I spent my own free time. I mean, she was studying foreign languages and I was on my couch playing video games and grinding out levels. Yikes.

"So we're done here?" I wiped my mouth roughly with my napkin, a little more excited than I should have been, perhaps, to get moving.

"Not quite," Thea said, and I watched with quiet dismay as she picked up her chopsticks again. "I just ordered takeout is all. Keep eating, it'd be a shame to let this go to waste. And we can't take out those dumplings anyway, they aren't any good when you reheat them."

I couldn't hide my confusion, and I sat there for a good few seconds, fiddling with my chopsticks. "Sorry. I'm – I guess I'm baffled, Thea."

"What's there to be baffled about?" She leaned one forearm on the table, then flicked her chopsticks out deftly to pick up a slice of ginger beef. "I'm just taking my best boy out on a lunch date is all."

I must have reddened a little, because hey, it was always nice to hear that my boss thought I was doing a good job. She laughed softly. I opened and closed my mouth, looking for something to say, but mercifully, Thea picked up and filled the silence for me.

"Oh, fine," she said, chewing thoughtfully on

the beef. She swallowed, took a small swig of her tea, then set her utensils down. "What I ordered, that's part of what we need for setting up our meeting. It's always going to be something different, depending on the entity. Each one has its own wants and desires, and you have to make an offering lovely enough for it to be lured to our plane, or at least to convince it to open a door to its own."

"So the offering is orange chicken."

Thea tutted. "Not in this case. Plus this place doesn't even do orange chicken. Although it depends on the entity, like I said. There was one that just wanted frozen hotdogs." She patted at the corner of her mouth with a napkin, eyes distant with remembrance. "No condiments. Didn't even ask for them to be cooked. Just wanted them frozen."

None of that explained much of anything at all, but there wasn't time to probe further. The waitress showed up, presenting Thea with a large bag of – something, along with the check. True to her promise, Thea picked up the tab, swatting my hand away when I offered to split the bill. I scratched at the back of my hand and muttered my thanks.

The waitress sorted the check, then came back with exactly two fortune cookies, presented lovingly on a brass serving dish.

"Now," Thea said. "I did say that they don't do Americanized Chinese food here, but some things are expected, so they still do the fortune cookies. Customers can be funny like that."

She picked one up, cracked it open in a single hand, then pulled out a slip of paper. She chuckled after reading it, then tucked her fortune into her breast pocket. "I'm pretty sure that was a song lyric," she said, patting at her pocket. "How about yours?"

I eyed the cookie suspiciously. I never did subscribe to anything involving superstition, fortunetelling, or divination, but what harm was there in playing along? It was just a mundane urban ritual. Just a fortune cookie, I told myself.

They made these little guys in a factory somewhere, with fortunes probably scoured from the web and printed out by some bored interns. It wasn't like Thea was shoving a soothsayer in my face, begging me to have my fortune told. And weirdly, yes, I still felt this apprehensive even after learning about the Veil, even knowing that some of this divination stuff was actually true. Sorry, can't tell you which. Trade secret.

"Fine," I said, perhaps a little mopier about it than I should have been. I picked up the cookie in one hand and crushed it, the way Thea did, except in my case it just splintered and crumbled all over the pristine red tablecloth. Damn. After I'd made so much effort not to spill anything over lunch, too.

Yet when I opened my fist, that's all there was in the palm of my hand: shards and crumbs of fortune cookie. No slip of paper to be found. No fortune.

"Um. Well that's – ominous." I meant it as a joke, but somehow saying it out loud drove a tiny sliver of dread into my chest.

Thea clapped her hands together, seemingly tickled. She shrugged, then made the worst possible joke she could have in that moment.

"That's the way the cookie crumbles."

Is it possible, I ask you, for someone who isn't a dad to make a dad joke? I'd like to know.

Minutes later we were making our way down the block, Thea all but gleaming in her pantsuit, looking out at the streets of Valero through a pair of aviators that somehow made her look even more executive than executive. I trailed after her like a hobo in my wrinkled jeans and jacket, squinting against the sunlight. Hey, I didn't know I'd be working so long that day, all right?

The bag of whatever it was from the Seven Dragons rustled as Thea carried it along on our little sojourn. She didn't ask me to bring it for her, and I didn't dare to ask lest she go on another of her circuitous "Did you know that tea is from China" lectures. I'd find out soon enough, anyway, except that instinctively I knew that I'd only have more questions as the afternoon stretched on. She stopped in front of a store just some blocks from the restaurant, and I knew I was right.

I looked up at the sign. "This is a bodega."

"Yes," she said, her face neutral. Those sunglasses really did a lot to hide her expression.

I cocked my head, then looked around. Absolutely nothing mystical at all about this place, but I shrugged and relented. "So – more reagents?"

Thea smiled. "You got it. I know it isn't quite as magical as you might have expected," she said, waving her one free hand in the air, waggling her fingers as she said the word. "But it works."

This time I didn't bother hiding my sigh. She laughed again, and I followed her into the store. Minutes more later we were back out on the streets again. She had picked up some of those little tea candles, a box of chalk, a water for herself, and a juice box for me. I was thirsty, and in need of sugar, don't judge.

At this point Thea took out her phone, peering at a map of the neighborhood to look for – well, whatever it was we were looking for. I tried to be cool about peeking over her shoulder, but she caught me out pretty quickly and chuckled it off.

"Hold on there. We're getting close."

"Another shopping expedition?"

"Very funny, Graves. No. We're looking for the entity's tether. It's like their signature in this realm, how we know we can access them from a physical location."

"Huh." I rubbed my chin, noticing that I'd been awake long enough to grow a faint bit of stubble. "So like an address."

Thea stopped mid-stride, then favored me with a wry smile. "Yes, actually, exactly like an address." She snuck another glance at her phone, then cocked her head over to the right. "This way."

I followed for a few more steps before asking the obvious. "I mean clearly this entity's address isn't just on your maps app, right?"

"Again: very funny. No, I'm looking for a specific brick wall. You'll understand when we get there." She poked her head down a particular alley, one that was shrouded in darkness despite the light of the noon sun, then slipped her phone back into her pocket. "Right. This is the place."

We stepped into the alley, the smell of it dank and musty, and maybe the burgeoning darkness of it should have made me nervous, but since I'd learned how to step, something about shadows soothed me, somehow. I knew I was safer with them nearby since I could always hoof it and find an exit. Which was almost what I did, mind you, when Thea pulled out a knife.

"Whoa." I backed away, my hands in the air. "Hey. Whoa."

Thea blinked at me, then lowered the knife, sputtering apologetically. "Oh God. Sorry. I forgot. I know you have a thing about these now."

I scratched at my chest, maybe unconsciously, my scar itching and burning as I eyed the knife. There wasn't much light in the alleyway, but whatever sun made it in there still caused the edge of the blade to glint in a way that made me a little too uncomfortable.

"Part of the process," Thea said, her voice softer and lower, adjusted to be reassuring. "Trust me on this." She set the knife carefully down on the ground, as if to assure me further, then placed both the Seven Dragons takeout and the bag from the bodega down as well. She got to work, sitting on her haunches, not seeming to care at how close her flawlessly white pants were to the filth of the alley.

"I'm guessing we've got the right spot?"

"Yep," Thea said, flipping open the box of chalk. She cocked her head at the near wall, gesturing at something there. "See for yourself."

I wasn't sure how I hadn't noticed, but something was marked on the wall, not quite in the spray-painted softness of the graffiti left there, but with a more definitive kind of precision, sharp edges and perfect lines deliberately placed, almost as if made with a stencil. I couldn't tell what it was exactly, this octagon with its criss-crosses of lines through the center, but I can tell you that it looked arcane and mysterious enough for me to buy Thea's story about tethers.

She huffed as she began sketching something out on the ground. "Truthfully," she said, "I had all these supplies back in my office." She scratched a few more lines into the asphalt, then looked up at me, grinning. "But where's the fun in that? This way we got to go on a little field trip together."

I smiled and shook my head. It had been an interesting afternoon, to say the least, and watching as she sketched out more symbols in chalk, I couldn't help but think that it was about to get even more interesting. She incanted under her breath, her lips moving as she went.

The drawing on the ground was starting to take shape, a loose collection of sigils and glyphs I didn't recognize from any language, all arranged in a ring. Thea drew a circle around the entire thing, as if to close it, then rummaged through her pockets for a lighter. She set the tea candles at specific intervals, then lit them.

"Okay," she said, getting up and brushing her hands against each other, patting off the chalk dust. "Story time. Sometimes it isn't enough to use incantations or hand gestures to get the magic flowing, especially for bigger projects like this. We're opening a doorway to another plane, after all. Knock knock. That takes more power, and that needs a circle."

My eyes widened at the thought of it. "So is that why cults exist? In terms of ritual magic, I mean. Bigger circles, not just of symbols like the stuff you drew, but actual circles of people?"

Thea looked up and tilted her head. "To a point, yes. You'd need a large enough group of like-minded people to get something going, or failing that, a large enough circle. For best results, both. It's the beauty of magic. It's like a built-in failsafe." She dusted her hands off some more, then laughed.

"I mean who ever heard of a giant summoning circle? The logistics alone. Still," she said, bending over to pick up the takeout bag. "That's the kind of stuff we don't want happening. Big circles, or big groups of people? All that energy and psychic ability directed towards the same goal? That's how you get an apocalypse going."

A squeaking from the corner of the alley called my attention. I grimaced at the sight of so many rats rushing for the darkness, even in broad daylight. Thea only shrugged. "They're still discombobulated after Resheph's death. Don't mind it, Dustin. It only takes time."

She stuck one hand into the takeout bag, retrieving, of all things, another fortune cookie. This wasn't explaining anything for me at all. Thea noticed my confusion and piped up again.

"Like I said, different entities, different tastes. This one likes Chinese restaurant fortune cookies. I wish I could tell you why."

Cookie in hand, she thrust her arm out over the circle, crumbling it into dust, letting the pieces fall into the chalk drawing. Then she picked up the knife and held her hand out again.

"And their tastes and reagents can change, but it's pretty unanimous that every entity expects a little bit of blood."

Before I could protest, Thea had poked the

knife into the tip of her thumb. Blood welled up immediately, a big enough drop that I could see it fall and splash onto the cement. It hissed, then smoked.

Something changed in the alley just then. Perhaps it went colder. Maybe it became darker, and I knew I didn't imagine the way the hairs on the back of my neck were standing on end, electric. And that strange chittering definitely wasn't there before.

Thea dropped the knife and picked up the takeout bag, her lips moving, but her mouth making no sound. Another incantation. I kept staring, waiting for her to say something audible, when a low humming emanated from the wall. The symbol on the bricks was gone. In fact, most of the wall was missing, replaced by a pulsing, silvery oval.

"A gateway," Thea said. "Your very first one." She beamed proudly. I looked at the portal uncertainly, then swallowed.

Thea beckoned, one hand lugging a plastic bag stuffed with fortune cookies, the other waving for me to step through the shimmering gossamer doorway. There was no backing out of this now.

"Come on, Dust. She's waiting." Thea smiled encouragingly. "Time to say hello."

Chapter 6

Magical transportation is an unusual concept, the kind of thing that needs to be expcrienced to be truly understood. I still haven't had tons of practice with shadowstepping, mainly because I've never had to stay inside of the darkness for very long. Not that I would want to. It could get bizarre inside the Dark Room, the name I've given the eerie dimension I have to traverse every time I shadowstep.

The shadows are cold, and it's hard to breathe. And there are different shades of dark, if you can believe that. Sometimes, in the scant seconds it takes me to walk from one shadow to the next, I fancy that I can see things moving in the black ethers. But the worst is the silence. When you're in that swirling chaos of darkness and shade, and you realize for the first time that you can't hear a single thing – not even the sound of your own voice as you scream in fresh terror – it cuts a little notch out of your soul.

Strange, I know, that someone should be so apprehensive of their own powers, but the Lorica taught us to respect those elements that were out of our control. And the world hiding behind shadow, that was a whole lot of stuff that was out of my hands. All I could do was accept the rules of that other dimension, to adjust to its realities. It was the same approach that I kept in mind when we entered the gossamer portal.

The gateway Thea and I stepped through was unnerving, to say the least. There was an immediately different quality to it, not the bleak silence and blackness of the Dark Room, but this odd feeling of thickness. Viscosity, maybe. The gossamer portal offered some resistance as we moved through it, forcing us to walk as if in slow motion. Even Thea seemed to have some trouble, forcing herself forward through what felt like an invisible barrier. Ever been in a Halloween haunted house? That was kind of what it felt like. Like walking through spiderwebs.

What awaited us on the other side was no more comforting. Dimness, all around, not quite like the dreary black of the shadows I'd become familiar with, but its own kind of pervasive dark. There were no fires here, magical or otherwise, like at the Lorica, only unseen sources of a sickly green light, cast over the entirety of the immense room. The white of Thea's clothing turned into a pale, diseased jade, the same color as the huge swaths of silk draping from the ceiling.

Did I not mention the silk? In the gloom the long, flowing sheets seemed to shift and billow, fluttering in the large, windless chamber we had found on the other end of the portal. In the stillness of the atmosphere, the sound of chittering was all the more disconcerting, no breeze blowing, but the noise of it like wind trailing through reeds. And all about us the thick, cloying smell of incense, of nothing specific, only a scent of something ancient and steeped in ritual.

That was all there was in the chamber, or this realm, to be more specific. I was just about to open my mouth, question at the ready, when Thea nodded to the far end of the darkness. The silks streaming from the ceiling parted, like curtains on a theater stage about to reveal something dramatic, something game-changing.

A woman sat behind the silks, bare-chested and beautiful, at least from the parts of her face that I could see. Her eyes were bound in the same whisper-light cloth that adorned the rest of the chamber, a kind of strange ceremonial veil. Her hair might have been a very silvery blonde, so close to white, her lips full, and slightly parted to show wet, white teeth. But in the strange, eldritch glow of the room, everything seemed greenish and ghoulish, and so she sat there unmoving, a statuette in jade.

She perched on an unusual sort of stool or throne, its legs segmented and decorated in all manner of hoops and bangles, fine furniture encrusted with jewels. The adornments matched those hung across her chest to cover her breasts, layers and layers of chains and little gemstones, even her bare arms and wrists and fingers glittering with gold.

"Wow," I muttered under my breath, marveling at the sight. Yet my attention wandered and returned to the woman's chair, so strange and alien it was. I wondered why it had eight legs.

That is, until two of them moved of their own accord.

"Come into my parlor," the woman said, her voice barely above a whisper. She chuckled, a distant rasping noise that made the silks in the hall tremble with every exhalation.

My first entity, Thea said, and here she was, this beautiful, terrible creature who was half woman, half spider, and she wanted us to come closer.

"Very funny, Arachne," Thea said, in a voice that spoke of some familiarity, but also caution, and maybe a hint of deference.

This woman, this Arachne, she tittered in response, the sound of it twittering across the chamber, making it seem like the noise was coming from all about us. She lifted a pale hand to her mouth, drawing attention to her wounded pout.

"It isn't my fault that you humans are so prone to celebrating my kind in your literature." She brought her fingers closer, examining her nails, sightless eyes somehow seeing through the silks wrapped over her face. "There was that famous man you had, this bard, they called him. What did he write, now? 'What tangled webs we weave?'" She tittered again. The silks – no, her webs, that was clear to me now – shivered and shook as she laughed, as if they were connected to her physically.

"Shakespeare," Thea said. "He was talking about how humans are prone to making things complex, whether with lies or other complications." She spoke deliberately, I noticed, like she was taking care to be informative without being condescending, her tone different from the one she used to regale me with stories about orange chicken and chop suey.

That's when it dawned on me. Thea was nervous. I'd never seen this side of her before, and in all honesty it made me fidgety, too. If my boss, a powerful, high-ranking sorceress of the Lorica itself had reason to be fearful of this entity, how was I supposed to feel? What had she gotten me into?

"That's why we're here," Thea continued. "There's lots of tangling going on, but not enough unraveling. We need clarity, Arachne. We need your help."

"We," the spider woman said, her voice brightening with glee. Her head turned in my direction. I could feel her gaze boring into me. I swallowed and did my best not to fidget or shuffle my feet.

"And who have you brought me today?" The soft rustle of her silks murmured through the chamber as she moved just the faintest bit closer, her jewelry tinkling like tiny bells. "Is this your offering?"

I repeat. What had Thea gotten me into?

Thea cleared her throat. "Not at all, Arachne. This is my protege. My apprentice, if you will. He is not an offering. He is not meant for consumption." I looked at her, aghast, waiting for her to chuckle and indicate it was a joke, but Thea's face was deathly serious. She was speaking plainly, specifically to avoid confusing this creature, in words that couldn't be misinterpreted.

I looked over my shoulder. The gossamer portal was still there. I measured the distance between my body and the gateway, and between myself and the spider on her throne. I knew I was fast enough to run if I had to, but I had to wonder if Arachne could be even faster. I glimpsed up at the ceiling, and at the canopy of silks that now looked so much like a net waiting to be dropped over us.

Arachne laughed, a full, throaty sound that caused her myriad jewels to jingle and glint in the dull light.

"Such a formal tone you use with me, Thea. Don't worry. I was making what you humans like to call a joke." Her lips parted in a smile. Her teeth were sharp. Far too sharp. "Such a pity. He certainly looks good enough to eat."

One of Arachne's legs snaked out, its length and its reach taking me by surprise, and it stroked against my jacket, running bristles against my shoulder. I realized that it was meant to be a friendly gesture, even flirtatious, maybe. Instinctively I knew that I would offend her by showing fear or revulsion, so I did that one thing I was really good at: I turned up the charm.

"I might look appetizing, but I promise you that I don't taste as delicious." I ignored the talon poking into my shoulder, the claws at the end of her leg, and gave her my best smile. "Surely your loveliness deserves a more appropriate treat."

She squealed. "It speaks!" Bangles and bracelets clinked as she clapped her hands, her body bounding as her legs skittered in excitement. "Oh, and such sweet words it brings me. Well done, Thea." She turned her head, the smile on her lips fading. "But as for sweet words and sweet treats. Have you a proper offering?"

"Of course," Thea said, giving me a sidelong glance. I could just detect a hint of approval in her expression. Maybe she was even a little proud of me. The plastic bag rustled as she held it out.

"Have the boy bring them to me." Arachne retrieved her leg, and now her frontmost limbs were twisting into the ground, the kind of body language I recognized as what a young girl might use to show shyness, hesitation. This was so fascinating. And, let's be real, utterly terrifying.

I accepted the bag from Thea, then strode forward. I tipped its contents out onto the floor before Arachne, just in front of her legs, and made a subtle bow. She squealed again. Her legs darted forward, sorting the cookies into piles, then separating them again, their plastic wrappers crinkling as she played with them as a child might fiddle with building blocks and marbles. I couldn't see her eyes, but I knew that they were gleaming.

"So many treats. So many fortunes. Where to start, where to start?" Her hands were up to her cheeks, which looked flushed even in the realm's sickly light. She turned to me again. "You. Sweetling. Which would you choose?"

I lowered my head. "I wouldn't presume, Arachne. The fortune you choose will always be the best."

And for a third time, the spider woman squealed. In a blur of black bristles and talons, one leg shot out, swiping at the cookie closest to my feet. I hardened my muscles, not daring to flinch, to even show discomfort. Arachne hummed pleasantly as the plastic fell away, and she broke the cookie apart in her human hands. It was odd to acknowledge that she functionally had ten limbs. I had so many questions, none of which I was allowed to ask. I stepped back to join Thea at her side. She nodded at me, and gave the smallest smile.

"You will soon embark on a business venture," Arachne pronounced, reading slowly and savoring each mouthful with ringing pride, like a child at a spelling bee. "Oh, how vague and clever and utterly pointless! Do your kind truly believe such drivel? Such whimsy in these little scrolls. You chose well, sweetling."

She secreted the fortune somewhere on her person, then crammed the broken cookies into her mouth, her fangs crushing them into dust. Arachne chewed noisily, shards of cookie flying past her lips as she spoke again. "Ask, then. Why have you come?"

"You know why." Thea clasped her hands together and lowered her head. "It is a grave matter. Someone is killing your kind."

"So I have heard."

Arachne sent out one hand, tugging at something invisible, until I saw that it was a gossamer strand, attached to the webs high in the ceiling. The faint chittering, the same sound we heard when we stepped into the portal started up again. I squeezed my fists, bit my tongue, and focused on the pain of my nails digging into my palms as tens, scores, then hundreds of spiders descended from the ceiling. I didn't dare steal a glance at Thea and only looked straight ahead, waiting with mounting panic as I saw that the spiders were pouring in from all corners of the room.

Some of the spiders swept across the fortune cookies still on the ground, snaring them with fine silks of their own before dragging them away into the darkness under Arachne's heaving thorax. I meditated on that spot of shadow, wishing I could just step in and whisk myself away.

"Someone has dared to kill an entity. That is what my children tell me."

Her children – hundreds of them – crawled up her arms, and for a moment it looked as if they had come bearing jewels. But I noticed that some of them did indeed have gemstones embedded in their backs. These rarer ones, the gilded spiders, crept closest to Arachne's ear, sitting quietly on her shoulder or draping themselves across her neck, each one its own link in a chain of gems. One dangled from her ear, a perfect, arachnid earring. She bent lower, as if to listen.

"They bring news to me. And much of it is ill."

"That's why we've come to you," Thea said, her voice steelier than before. I could tell she was pouring more conviction into it. Couldn't blame her. Arachne's children were still swarming around her, a huge, coalescing mass. One word from her and Thea and I would be as good as dead.

"This is a larger request than you thought, friend." Arachne held the silence, stretching it for emphasis. "I demand one of your baubles in exchange for my knowledge."

Her jewels. Thea wore so many of them that I knew she had enough to spare, but I also knew that her jewelry was precious to her. She had crafted and imbued each piece with arcane power herself. Like the opal I wore, nearly each one had its own enchantment, its own purpose. Thea nodded at me, selecting one of her larger rings. It didn't look any different than the others, but I had a suspicion that she had prepared for just such an occasion. This was probably a decoy, unensorcelled, just a mundane gift.

"Very well, Arachne." Thea worked the ring slowly off her finger, twisting it begrudgingly, making a great show of hesitation. "It pains me to do this, but I grant you one of my most precious stones."

And Arachne didn't squeal this time, but I could feel the delight emanating from her in waves. Even her children seemed more placid, less threatening than before.

No ceremony this time, no playful ploy to get Thea's protege to deliver the goods. A large spider descended on a single strand of web, collecting the ring from Thea's outstretched hand. She hardly seemed perturbed. The spider scuttled across the ground, then threw a line up to its mistress. Arachne received her emissary with gentle fingers, cradling it in both hands. She wore the ring on her left hand, turning her head this way and that, admiring it in the light.

"You already know that the manner of slaughter was magical," she said, her voice deeper, and taut. "That much would be clear, even to one as unlearned as your apprentice." Her unseen eyes glanced in my direction, and the smile she favored me with was oddly warm. "What I do know is that the murder was committed with the intent to siphon Resheph's power. Whether the murderer did so to add to his own strength, or to gain control over Resheph's dominion, I cannot say."

"Dominion? You mean rats?" Thea frowned. "Who needs rats?"

Arachne hissed, her legs adjusting, scraping against the stone floor as she reared herself up to her full, terrifying height. The spider half of her being was coming to fore. The green light of the chamber flickered, then everything seemed darker. The chittering of the spiders grew in volume and frequency, and all around us the silks in the hallway quavered as more, impossibly more spiders poured out of the darkness.

"Who needs rats?" Arachne said mockingly, her voice sing-song and high. "Some might say that my children are just like rats. Skulking in darkness, in the corners and the in-betweens. Vermin they may be, yes, but you belittle my brethren's children, even as you come to trade for the secrets that my offspring bring me."

"That wasn't our intention," Thea said. This time, despite her unwavering stance and her gaze, I knew that she was overcompensating.

"And yet you move to offend me," Arachne spat. "I should kill you where you stand. I should feed you to my young, have the millions of them rend the flesh from your bone."

Arachne skittered forward, the forbidding bulk of her body clearing the room in the blink of an eye. Her children moved with her, a carpet of spiders following wherever their queen led. Arachne's teeth were bared, and it wasn't the green light's doing anymore. Something viscous, the color of jade, was dripping down her teeth, past the corner of her mouth.

I don't know what came over me then. Blind idiocy, bravado, or madness, or maybe an innate desire to show my boss that I could perform in a real world, high-stress occupational situation. I stepped between Thea and the hulking mass of Arachne's body, mindful that each of her legs was the size and thickness of a spear, with the honed, pointed sharpness to match.

"Please," I started. "We didn't mean to anger you. We only came to receive your wisdom. I beg your forgiveness for us both. Don't let this ruin your temper, or tarnish your beauty."

Anticipation burned like fire under my skin as Arachne craned her head in my direction, but I knew I had hit my mark. The faintest hint of a smile crept into the corner of her lips, then faded just as suddenly.

"You are fortunate that you have brought this one to whisper sweet words to me, Thea. No blood shall be spilled today, but neither shall I tell you more. If I should learn anything else, I may deign to relay it to your apprentice."

She lowered herself gently, graceful in spite of the bulk of her thorax, then pressed her lips against my forehead. Her kiss was moist, and while the sensation of it burned on my skin, I knew she meant me no harm. And I could finally see her up close, and decipher what hid behind the veil across her face. All eight of her eyes focused on me as she smiled. Three of them winked.

"Now that you are marked, my brood can more easily find you," Arachne said. "Tell your master here of anything that my children whisper in your ears." She retreated slowly, her gaze alternating between the two of us. "You may leave with your lives."

Finally, in a small voice, Thea spoke. "Thank you, Arachne."

I didn't need to be told twice, already knowing that I'd be getting more visitations from this strange spider queen and her horrific offspring. I couldn't remember whether it was me or Thea who reached the gossamer portal first, only that we were both relieved to find ourselves back in the alleyway, clutching our knees and panting from the effort of sprinting. Thea's forehead gleamed. She was sweating, and shuddering.

"That was her," I panted, wiping at my upper lip. "From mythology. The woman Athena turned into a spider. She's real."

"They all are," Thea said, patting at her forehead with her sleeve, her hand faintly trembling. "They live in the unseen spaces, like spiders. In the corners. Here and there, between the cardinal directions. Anywhere you aren't looking, there they are."

My breath returned to me in gasps. The dust in the alley choked at my lungs, and I couldn't wait to get out, to breathe in the relatively fresher air of the city.

"Come on, Thea. We should go."

"One minute," she said, rubbing her knees. "Just – just give me one minute."

In spite of the darkness, by the timbre of Thea's voice alone, I could tell something was wrong. It was tough to see her so shaken by our encounter, her perfect surface splintered and cracked. Thea was someone I looked up to. She saved my life, once. She was a hero. It stung to see her so defeated.

Thea lifted her hand to her face again, rubbing her sleeve under one eye. I looked away, pretending that I didn't see her tears.

Chapter 7

It was dark by the time I got home. Actually, let me clarify that statement. It was already dark by the time we'd gotten out of the alley. Thea said that being in Arachne's domicile had done something to compress time, so that the minutes we had spent there were hours in the real world.

I'd waited long enough for her to get a ride, making sure she was fine to get along on her own. She offered to drop me off, but I didn't want her knowing that I wasn't heading back to my apartment, but my other home – at least what I used to call home back when I was somehow even younger and dumber.

I hugged my elbows as I watched from the safety of the shadows in the garden, or whatever passed for a garden at the house where I grew up.

This had become a kind of ritual for me since I'd joined the Lorica, since the day someone tried to snuff my life out, which was part of the reason I didn't want Thea knowing. It wasn't healthy, she said, and damn it if she wasn't right.

The lights were on inside the living room as they always were this time of the evening, without fail. That was when the man who lived here started actually putting things together for dinner. Once he did that for his wife and son, but both of them had gone.

I craned my neck to get a better look at what he was preparing. Time was when he would make stuff from scratch, something comforting like a chicken pot pie, or a casserole on lazier nights. I guess things were different when you were on your own, when there was no one to please, no one to tell you how good your cooking was. I watched as the man, who had the same black hair as me, the same blue eyes, pulled out a flat box from the freezer.

"Not another frozen dinner," I muttered to myself, as if he could even hear, my words leaving my mouth in wisps of fog. "Come on, dad."

Norman – the name I never called him for fear of getting smacked upside the head – was a cheerier person, once. Things used to be great at home. He liked to build things. When the mood took him, sometimes he'd sit down and play video games with me. Sometimes he'd even kick my ass. And mom, she liked to tinker with old toys and bikes and machines, and to bake, and some weekends we'd all head down to the beach for a picnic. I always loved the smell of the ocean, the sound of surf. They reminded me of family, and home.

Things started to change when mom died. Cancer killed Diana Graves, and then it broke my father's heart. I must have been seventeen then. I did what I could to console him, to lighten the load, help around the house, you know, just keep him company. I couldn't say that it ever helped. Before things went south, he always used to say that I reminded him of my mother. Towards the end I think I began to remind him of her in all the wrong ways.

I wasn't the perfect son. I never said I was. Still it got to be too much, between the push and pull of him being angry with me for the littlest things, but still wanting me around, begging me not to move out when things got too tense between us. "I'll still visit," I told him. "I promise." I shuddered against the cold and smiled tightly. I always kept my promises.

Norman Graves was skinnier now, his face sallow, his eyes sunken a little further into his head than they should have been, but I knew I couldn't just walk in there, tell him I was sorry, that I wanted us to be a family of two again. The last time I visited there was an argument. I left angry. He'd never been happy with how I couldn't find something to do with myself, with my life, and the grandest irony was that now that I'd found something worth doing, I couldn't even tell him about it to make him proud of me for once.

That's why I knew that it weighed heavier on him, why he must have thought in some twisted section of his brain that it was his fault I ended up the way I did. That made it even harder to just knock on the door and announce myself. Ah, but that was the toughest part. I couldn't even do that, not when he was there when they lowered my body into the ground.

Where to start? It was some weeks ago, the same night I had it out with my dad. I didn't head back to my apartment right away, that shabby piece of shit I shared with those two roommates I didn't even like, but hey, you have a shitty job, or no job at all, you put up with shitty living conditions. I didn't know what possessed me to do so, but I took off and went to a park, just to walk around, to clear my head.

There were no joggers that night, as if everyone but me knew to steer clear of Heinsite Park. I saw a woman bent over a pond in the park, crying to herself, something about her dog. I went to help. I love dogs. And just as she was blubbering, explaining how little Sassy had fallen into the pond, something hard clubbed me across the back of the head.

When I came to I was in a dark room, strapped to a table, it felt like, what I now know must have been some kind of altar. Everything was dim, tinged with orange, like the only illumination was a whole bunch of candles.

And above me, all around me, were golden faces gleaming in the candlelight, people in bronze masks muttering, incanting. I tried to scream, but couldn't. They must have drugged me. They strapped me down by the chest, but didn't bother to bind my arms, like they were so confident I'd be too weak or doped up to fight back. They were almost right.

The dagger's edge flashed in the light, a ceremonial blade that was so ornate, its hilt and guard covered in curved spines, like tendrils, its pommel gleaming with a gem that looked disturbingly like a single eye. It must have been the drugs, but I found it strange, just then, that I had time to identify the dagger's different parts – who said video games were bad for you? – and to admire its craftsmanship. Then the hand holding the dagger brought it down.

So my life was complete garbage by then. No real job to speak of, a dad who, at the time, hated me, trash roommates, the works. But I didn't want to die, and the pain – the fucking, searing pain of that cold dagger burying its way into the meat of my body, that reminded me of how alive I still was, and how alive I still wanted to be. But the knife hit home, biting into its sacrifice, and the screaming pain in my chest crashed across my entire body like freezing water. Everything went black. For all intents and purposes, I died.

Except that I came to again. Just as well, or you wouldn't be here listening to this incredible tale of a near-jobless loser getting his redemption at the hands of the Lorica. I opened my eyes, and the first person I saw may as well have been an angel. That was when I met Thea for the very first time.

She had rescued me from the cultists, her and the team she'd brought from the Lorica. But the problem, she explained, was that the police had beaten them to it. The dagger hadn't fully killed me. It was meant to, but with the ritual interrupted, it had only put me into a kind of magic-induced torpor, numbing enough of my body's signals that I was fully a corpse by the time the cops came around.

The Pruitts, the dead god I found at their home, those were victims of supernatural circumstance, of arcane crime, in the exact same way that I was. One of the Lorica's Eyes – Romira, in fact – had found my body already shoved into a freezer, barely steps away from being buried six feet under.

The Lorica rescued me, pulling out all the stops to infiltrate the morgue and retrieve my body, somehow replacing it with a simulacrum that was convincing enough to show the authorities that one Dustin Graves was well and truly dead.

They buried that copy of me in the ground. My

father watched and wept as they lowered it into a hole, and I watched from the shadow of a tree as he cried over a mannequin, unable to tell him that I was fine, that I loved him, that I was alive.

And that was the price of this second life I had received, that the Dustin Graves I once was could no longer exist. I had to excise all parts of my routine from my former life, old haunts, what few acquaintances I had. I have to admit, I was mildly happy that my idiot roommates had to scramble to find some other loser to start making rent again.

The only problem was Norman, and that was a sizeable issue, too. I couldn't just stride through the front door with a "Hey dad, been alive this whole time, what's good?" I could tell his emotions were fraying as it was. "A secret society of wizards saved me. I'm not actually dead, also, I can do magic, and so can my coworkers." I mean, where would you even start? He didn't need the walking corpse of his zombie son strolling in and fucking his life up any further.

But there has to be a way, I thought, even as I watched him peering through the microwave window, waiting for his stroganoff whatever to finish cooking. Maybe a series of notes, or maybe someone from the Lorica could ease him into it. Maybe I could beg one of the alchemists to brew up a potion of forgetfulness, if that even existed, just to make everything the way it was again.

But I had no answers then, and neither did

Thea, who had promised to help me find the people who tried to kill me. I sighed, stepping into the shadows in the garden, then breathed easier when I stepped out of the darkness directly onto the sidewalk, safely out of view of our old house. And the job offer was so attractive to begin with, being asked to become a Hound.

"How would you like to find your own killer?" she asked.

Fuck yeah. Which wasn't how I responded exactly, but you get the gist of it. And it came with decent benefits too, and a bigger paycheck than I'd ever gotten from any of my godawful jobs. Sure, it's the age of the internet and everything, but somehow nobody in Valero was ever hiring, especially not some kid with a scattershot job history, no recommendations, and oh, no degree. I might have mentioned it quietly before, but I'll restate it now for emphasis: the Lorica damn near saved my life, then turned it around, and then some.

The paycheck was even enough for me to get a shitty apartment of my own. No roommates, even. It was no coincidence that it was walking distance from my dad's place. I could afford a little more now, and considering how things ended between us, I figured it was good for me to have the freedom to check in on him every now and again.

My place was a tiny little studio in this block of apartments meant for college students, so it was livelier, well, noisier than I would have liked, but it was a place to keep my bed, and my unfortunate growing collection of gaming consoles. Don't judge, my life could get super stressful. You try getting murdered some time.

Sure, I kid about it, but almost every day I would think of the same small set of questions. Who would want good old Dustin Graves dead? I had few friends, and no enemies, as far as I knew. Why did the cultists single me out? As I began the slow climb home, up on the third floor, I slapped my forehead.

Why didn't I ever remember to do groceries?

Because I'd been away for a while. At least I had an excuse this time. But I'd been so tired from working straight through the night, then accompanying Thea to meet the entity. All that Chinese from lunch had burned off, too.

I groaned, thinking of how much more convenient it would have been to just pop into my place, heat something up, wolf it down, then pass out for twenty-four hours. Suddenly dad's frozen stroganoff dinner was sounding pretty tempting.

I turned around and dragged my exhausted ass down the street, down a couple of blocks to the nearest source of food my frazzled brain could reliably find. There was this awesome place further down that did these incredible steak burritos, but who had the energy? I settled, mentally, for a burger. Salty, greasy, filling, just

90

what the doctor ordered.

This place had been one of my regular haunts even before the whole human sacrifice thing, actually, but the staff changed so frequently that nobody ever stuck around long enough to remember me. Plus keeping my stubble and growing out a longer hairstyle made for a surprisingly effective disguise.

Good thing too, because the burgers were incredible. It was one of those places that was halfway between a proper restaurant and a fast food joint, the kind that tried to be hip and still serve the good stuff. There were neon signs plastered all over the Happy Cow – grim name, I know – in a kind of throwback to the twenties diner aesthetic that was supposed to appeal to us young folk.

The Happy Cow didn't know what it wanted to be, in short, and the floors were almost always a little oily and slippery, but the food was top notch, so I couldn't complain. And the lighting was kind of terrible, so much that not even the manager remembered me, probably because I still took the extra precaution of wearing a hooded jacket.

I ordered a double cheeseburger, a Coke, and both a large fry and a large onion ring because screw you, I was starving. I tucked myself into a corner seat, one of those high stools where you ate facing the window, maybe because I was daring anybody to judge me for the giant heap of food I was about to demolish.

Didn't remember chewing very much, only that it was all delicious, the hot, juicy patties with the edges singed just a little, the crunch of fresh vegetables and the warmth of a lightly toasted bun, and all that melted cheese. That was all I really needed in life, you know? Cows, carbs, cheese. I knew that as long as I ticked off all the major food groups, my body was going to be fine.

But as I sucked down the last of my Coke, somehow still remembering enough of my manners to pat at the corner of my mouth, I realized that something was off, and not just the rodents. I watched aghast as a darting, frenetic procession of rats made its way from across the street over to the Happy Cow's dumpster. Gross. My skin crawled at the idea of this happening all over Valero. How long were they going to be disoriented by Resheph's death?

Yet it wasn't the rats that bugged me. I looked around. Everyone in the restaurant was busy doing their own thing. A girl with tattooed sleeves and a septum piercing ignored her boyfriend while she tapped at her phone. An older bearded man sat alone, dissecting his burger, separating bun from patty to apply just the right sized dollops of ketchup and mustard, then putting it back together again. Everything seemed fine, but I just knew that it wasn't.

Okay, I told myself. Play it cool. You'd think by now I'd have been smart enough to arm myself, but I wasn't exactly a fighter. It'd be nice to have a knife on your person, sure, but someone could wrestle it away and use it against you. And I was nowhere near the point where I'd been taught any proper defensive magic – or offensive stuff, for that matter, but even if I could cast something I knew the Lorica wouldn't take kindly to me frying people with lightning bolts. So I dumped my trash and walked out of there as calmly as I could, like nothing was wrong, like I hadn't caught a whiff of something in the air.

I hadn't made it two blocks when I noticed the two men on my tail. One was just as tall as me, the other even taller, and beefier. I knew just from the cursory glance over my shoulder that I wasn't built to take on even one of them. I also knew that heading straight back to my apartment, as tempting as that was, would only show them where I lived, if they didn't know already.

Damn it. What did they want? Call me paranoid but something in my gut told me that this wasn't just a mugging in the making. These people had something to do with the Pruitt murders, maybe, or the cultists. Or both. The Black Hand.

The scar on my chest began to itch. I stuck my hands deeper down in my jacket pockets and kept walking, turning down the wrong way in hopes of shaking them off, maybe stepping into a shadow before they could see. But they were too fast, and they were gaining on me, too.

Persistent. Okay. Next corner, I told myself. The exact next corner, and I would step into the shadow of the nearest tree or lamppost, then try, for the first time, to emerge all the way back home. I almost didn't care at that point that I might end up half-stepped into a fire hydrant. Whoever these guys were, they had no plans of stopping.

I looked over my shoulder one last time as I approached the next block, making another left turn as I noticed that only one man was still pursuing me, the taller, broader one. Where the hell did the other guy go? It didn't matter. I turned the corner, my eyes darting wildly for the first shadow I could find –

And bumped straight into the missing man. I gasped at the sight of him, at the odd pallor of his skin, the marble smoothness of his cheeks. I raised my hands, I don't know, I guess to show that I didn't mean him harm, and in some hope that he wouldn't harm me in return. He mirrored my pose with a chuckle, a low, musical sound, his eyes black and twinkling.

"Whoa there," he said. "Didn't mean to bump into you," he continued, with the exact tone of someone who meant to do just that.

"What do you want?" I demanded, glancing over my shoulder again, preparing to shadowstep, just as I caught sight of the taller man closing in on us.

"Just to talk. Stay a while, Dustin."

I froze. The man knew my name. These people had their sources, the way the Lorica had its Eyes. Someone was watching. Always watching.

The man grinned, his smile splitting his face and revealing a pair of sharp, unnaturally long canines.

"The night is young," he said, in a voice that was at once husky, and hungry. "Let's get to know each other."

Chapter 8

Somehow the pale man had pushed me up against the wall without even touching me. He had this way of invading, no, bypassing my personal space. It was a creeping sort of presence that latched on and mesmerized me, long enough at least that the taller man had time to join our huddle.

"Look, Gil," the pale man said. "Look what I found. He was gonna run away. He's one of those – what does the Lorica call them again." He cocked an eyebrow, then bent in, smiling. "Hounds?"

My heart pounded. Whoever these people were, they knew about the Veil, which narrowed things down in a bad way. My hunch must have been correct. These assholes worked for the Black

Hand.

I opened my mouth to speak, but I couldn't say anything without incriminating myself. The taller man – Gil – grunted anyway. He stepped closer, looming over the two of us, and I pressed further against the wall, as if there was anywhere else to go. This man was powerfully built, dark and swarthy, with thick eyebrows and a beard that only pronounced his menace. Yet when he spoke, the steady calm of his voice surprised me.

"Get it over with. Just beat what you need out of him and we can get out of here."

"Aww, Gil, you're no fun. Stray little puppy's out on his own when he shouldn't be." The pale man hooked a finger under my necklace, tugging on it lightly the way Bastion would, and it sent ice down my spine, this awful mix of indignation and fear. His hand made contact with my neck as he toyed with the leather thong. His fingers were cold, and I knew it wasn't only because of the night air.

"I don't know nothing about no Lorica," I blurted out, too eager to save my own skin. It was the best thing I could think to say, and besides, it bought me time to study my options.

The pale man drew his face back, then grinned again. In the moonlight, his fangs gleamed. "Our new friend is a bit of a liar, Gil."

The man called Gil rolled his eyes and grunted again. "You do this all the time. Stop playing with your food and get on with it."

"Your what?" Did he just call me food?

"Don't scare him, Gil." The fingers stopped playing with my necklace, then moved on to press lightly against my skin. "That's not what we're here for. Although now that you mention it, I wouldn't mind a little snack." He bent in, inhaled sharply, and grinned again. "He's so hot, too."

I cringed at his touch, still unsure of what to do, and somehow my brain turned to humor to defuse the situation. "Thanks," I said, my nails digging into the wall behind me. "I try."

The pale man laughed. "Oh, and cocky. I like this one." His fingers pushed deeper against my skin, the edges of his nails digging. "I meant your blood."

"Yeah," I said. "Fuck this."

I brought my knee up against the pale man's crotch, as hard and abruptly as I could. As far as I was concerned there was no shame in taking every advantage I could find in a fight, not if it meant saving myself from a hypothetical vampire.

The breath rushed out of him in a rough gasp and he doubled over long enough to let go of me, and far back enough to cast a shadow on the ground. I stepped into it, more thrilled than I had ever been to walk into the gloom of the Dark Room, and emerged several feet away.

Gil looked around wildly, roared, then shoved the other man hard in the chest. "I fucking told you, didn't I?"

The vampire stumbled, but only just. "Gil," he choked out, between gasps of pain and stilted chuckles. "Did you see that? He wants to make this a game. A chase it is then."

"Not this shit again," Gil said. "Get your balls back together and come on."

I ran. It hardly mattered which direction I was heading at this point, only that I pushed into the darkest places I could possibly lead these psychos to. Funny how that worked, how that sort of reckless behavior was what got me killed in the first place, but it was exactly what I needed to save me this time around. I headed for the place where I was abducted before my murder. I made a beeline for Heinsite Park.

Footsteps stamped the pavement behind me. I didn't dare turn to check how far away the two were, only focusing on looking straight ahead and making a mad dash for the darkness. It was that time of night when there weren't a lot of people around, too, but what few there were either avoided my gaze entirely or stared pointedly. I didn't care. I just wanted to get out of there unscathed, with all my blood right where it belonged: inside of my body.

The park was just up ahead. Theoretically I could have stepped into any of the shadows leading up to that point, but that would have limited my options for exits. This way I could operate by line of sight, and the wide expanse of Heinsite Park gave me plenty of choices and opportunities for escape. If only I had the presence of mind to dress in darker colors. I really liked black, too, just that I decided against it, oh, two nights ago.

It struck me then, that it had been that long since I'd had a change of clothes, a shower, or hell, a decent night's sleep. I shrugged those thoughts away, making a mental promise to always, always, always dress in black in the future, especially for excursions and infiltrations. What the hell was I doing dressing in a light gray hoodie when I went to steal the Book of Plagues? I shook my head. Never again. And that was, of course, still contingent on whether I survived the night.

The cold air ripped at my lungs as I ran. I finally gave myself a second to glance over my shoulder, and my heart puttered when I saw that the two men were within leaping distance, the hypothetical vampire just paces ahead of the guy who looked like he could break me in half over his knee. Now or never. I picked my entry point – just under a nearby tree – and fixed on an exit, right by a dead lamppost, some twenty feet away. I stepped.

The chill of the night went chillier, and the cries of surprise from my pursuers went muted just as soon as I entered the shadows. Everything was muffled, as it always was, and chaotic, with the swirls of blackness enveloping, clouding my vision.

But what stood out to me was how much harder it was to breathe, a combination, I guessed, of how I'd been running and was naturally out of breath, and the fact that I was making a much longer step for the first time. I fought the doubt taking over me, any thought that I would fail to make the leap, because what use was successfully evading my pursuers if it meant I'd done so by shunting myself deep into a brick wall?

Moments later I emerged from the Dark Room. I could breathe again. The men's voices came from much further away. Good. I'd put some distance between us. I felt light-headed, disoriented, but at least I was safe, and – I patted at my limbs, at my face, just to be sure – probably in one piece. I gave myself a scant few seconds to catch my breath, then turned again to check on my stalkers, and yes, maybe I briefly considered taking just enough time to give them the finger.

The bigger man, Gil, was some fifteen feet away, where he should have been, but the other one was streaking towards me, his body a blur, a horrific silver arrow shooting unerringly in my direction, legs pumping, and one hand outstretched. When he was only a few feet away, I heard him snarl.

"No," I muttered. "No no no," a string of murmured panic as I turned around and ran into the nearest shadow I could find. How had he caught up to me so quickly? I heard him shout in frustration as I blinked out of view again, and this time I didn't even know where I was headed, only that it had to be away from him, away from them.

I stumbled through the Dark Room, through the shuddering mists, the shadows closing in on me, becoming heavier and heavier. And when I could no longer breathe, when the chill had sucked the air and the warmth from me, skin and bone, I tripped and fell headlong into the light.

Regaining my bearings, I looked around. I was still in the park, this time shifted several dozen feet away from the last point. Gil was hurtling towards me, the change in direction taking some wind out of his velocity, but his partner was nowhere in sight. I clenched my fists, testing my limits, but no go. I knew I couldn't shadowstep anymore. I was out of steam.

Crap. I summoned what strength I had left – zero sleep, a full stomach, and more numerous, much larger steps than I'd ever taken – and put one foot in front of the other. It was a spirited attempt to break into a full run, I thought, until the canopy of trees above my head started rustling.

Something pale sprang out of the darkness and crushed me, knocking the wind out of my lungs and sending me sprawling across the cement. I had scuffed up my knees, that was for sure, and there was a sharp pain in my elbow, but I knew that wouldn't matter much compared to what these lunatics had in store for me.

One of the man's knees dug into my breastbone.

"Can't. Breathe."

"Hmm?" the man said, feigning disinterest. "Sorry, I couldn't hear you over the sound of my balls breaking." He tugged at his hair, picking a leaf out of it, grimacing. "That was very sneaky of you."

"Not sorry," I sputtered out.

"Real cute." The man placed a hand, fingers splayed, across my chest. He was light, the weight of him barely noticeable as he straddled my body. Still, something in how he incapacitated me as easily as he would pin a child to the ground suggested that fighting my way out would end very, very painfully.

Heavy footsteps told me that Gil had finally caught up to us. He panted, wiping at his beard with the back of his hand, brows knitted in anger.

"He wants him alive," Gil said.

He? Who was he? Who wanted me alive?

"I know that," the man on top of me snapped. "Just – let me have this one. A tiny little snack." His lips parted, and this time I saw his canines descending, two inhumanly sharp fangs protruding from his top row of perfect teeth.

"So you – you really are a vampire," I stammered. He could probably feel my heart pounding under his hand.

The man rolled his eyes. "Brilliant deduction.

You made me work up a sweat, little Hound. Got me all thirsty. I just want to take a quick sip. Haven't had me some magical blood in a minute."

"We don't have time for this," Gil hissed, looking around like he was worried someone might see.

"Shush, Gil. Just a little bite." He smiled at me. "You don't mind, do you?" The man parted his lips, his teeth silver in the moonlight, and he bent down. His breath smelled like lilacs.

"Die in a fire," I grunted.

I struggled and bucked, and on reflex, my hand went to my throat, as if that could have been enough to protect me. But my fingers brushed against the leather thong of my necklace, and then against the opal dangling from it. I didn't even have time to think of anything to say, but the connection must have held up, because the transmission of thought and emotion was instantaneous, immediate.

"Fuck," I thought, in a flash of wild panic.

Thea's reply came lightning fast: "You dumb idiot."

Now, here was the thing about the Lorica's higher-ups, the executives, the Scions, call them what you like. They didn't like us grunts knowing exactly they could do in the arcane department. Knowledge is power, as the saying goes, and the smartest way to counter someone magically was to grasp what they were capable of, the way a less than scrupulous coach might go and record an opposing team's game or routine.

All I really knew of Thea was that she had perfected numerous spells, had a collection of enchanted baubles, and mainly specialized in an ability to magically manipulate light. Funny, that, how the two of us ended up working together, one walking in darkness, the other, a master of illumination.

I suppose I shouldn't have been entirely surprised, then, when a segment of the darkness above me brightened. A light, somewhere in the clouds. I gawped, almost forgetting that I was squirming under the hands of an undead thing that wanted me for a midnight snack. The shaft of light in the night sky grew brighter – yellower than the stars, and more luminescent, somehow – until I saw it for what it was. A pillar of brilliance, piercing the veil of dark, rocketing towards the earth from out of the atmosphere.

I wasn't sure how Thea did it, or how she knew my exact position, but the light must have reflected in my eyes because the vampire tilted his head curiously at my expression. Then he turned his face. The beam of light seemed almost solid against the velvet dark of midnight, and as it struck home it shone brightly against my skin, a puddle of warmth, familiar and comforting. I recognized it for what it was – sunlight. But the vampire was in the way –

And how he screamed.

I had never heard a man howl quite as hideously as the vampire did that night, and I don't ever want to hear anything like it again. The sunbeam was nothing more than a ray of warmth as it graced the earth, but against the vampire's face it might as well have been a flamethrower. I could smell his flesh as it sizzled and cooked under the light's touch, his cheek charred to cinders, his hair incinerating wherever the pillar made contact.

He shrieked in pain, the bone showing through what flesh had been flayed from his skull, and the screaming didn't stop when he covered his face with his hands. Within seconds the flesh had been burned from them, too, leaving ragged hanks of torn skin and skeletal fingers. I gagged, choking on the smell of cooked undead flesh, of burned hair. He rolled off me, crawling for shade and shelter, but the pillar of sun followed him like a searchlight. Thea wasn't fucking around.

The vampire rolled on the ground, shielding his face with the sleeve of his leather jacket – finally, some reprieve. I was starting to feel bad for him, almost, this thing that was so intent on taking my blood. Gil looked at me menacingly, then warily up at the pillar of light, then at his comrade lolling about on the ground. He shook his head and cursed under his breath, his decision made, and he enveloped the vampire with his body, guarding him from the sunbeam.

"I told you," he said, scolding the vampire, "but did you listen? Do you ever listen?"

"Fuck off," the vampire cried, half-whimpering, half-screaming. His voice was different now, issuing from his blistered mouth.

I took my chance to run. Gil was the slower of the two, and whatever he was, he didn't have the insane acrobatics that the vampire could resort to, so I went on foot as far as I dared, hitting the edge of Heinsite Park before, for good measure, stepping into the shadows and shunting my way across the street. When I was far enough that I couldn't hear the vampire wailing, far enough that I knew it was safe to sit and breathe, I took some time under the shadows of an office building.

It was a little trick I picked up some time back: by standing perfectly still in the darkness, I could sometimes almost pass myself off as invisible, as if a portion of me receded into the Dark Room. That wouldn't have helped against the vampire, of course, since I was sure he could have still smelled me or sensed my body heat.

After catching my breath, I turned my attention to a new, unpleasant task: reporting in to Thea. I bit my lip as I raised two fingers to my necklace. Even before making contact I already knew she was going to be unhappy. Kind of an understatement.

"Fine mess you got yourself into," Thea said. "A damn, fine mess."

I hugged my knees. "Sorry. And thanks for saving me. And sorry again."

"You're lucky everything came flooding in when you called. A vampire. A vampire, Dustin!"

"I know. I'm sorry."

"Why didn't you call me earlier?"

I didn't think to, or maybe there was that certain fear of being yelled at by an authority figure, which, in retrospect, would still have been leagues better than being kidnapped by Sir Pervert von Vampire and his hairy companion.

"I don't know," was all I said.

"I told you about going around alone at night, didn't I?"

I sighed. Thea clearly wasn't going to let up on this one. "I was starving. I just went for a burger. That's all."

She scoffed. "We can't have you roaming on your own from now on. I'm not taking any more risks with you."

"Wait, what?" Dread crept up my spine, or maybe it was the coldness of the brick against my back, but I knew that whatever was coming next wasn't going to make me happy. "What do you mean?"

"It isn't safe for you to stay alone in your apartment anymore. I need you to pack your things."

"Wait." I blinked. "Am I moving in with you?"

Telepathically, Thea guffawed. "Try again."

I felt like someone had dumped a bucket of ice

water all over me. "You're not asking me to move into HQ, are you?" The line was silent. "Hello? Thea?"

She didn't answer. I couldn't tell you how I knew, but I swear I felt her smiling.

Chapter 9

"You're kidding," Romira said, eyes wide as saucers. "You have to live here, right in HQ?"

I nodded, then shrugged. I was as much at a loss for words as anyone. When I made it back to my apartment that night, I got another transmission from Thea. She had settled down by then, telling me that I could spend one last night at the apartment, but that I was to report promptly to the office the following morning, and to take my valuables with me.

"And several changes of clothes," she said. "Enough to last you an indefinite period."

I wasn't sure what she meant by that exactly, which was why I was standing in the kitchenette with a duffle bag full of clothes and toiletries. Truthfully I didn't own very much. Having to start my life over showed me that humans actually didn't need a whole lot to survive. All I really had were T-shirts, jeans, socks, some underwear, a couple of jackets, and a few pairs of sneakers.

Everything I needed was in that bag. Well, save my consoles, television, and desktop computer, but Thea said that she had some people working on moving those over as well. I was a hundred percent sure this special treatment was going to make me extra popular at work.

"I'm surprised she even let me stay another night, if I'm honest," I told Romira. She scratched the side of her nose at that, turning away. I tilted my head. "What?"

"Well," she started. "Did she mention that you were going to be safe?"

"She did." In fact, Thea said that she was going to have a couple of Hounds keep watch over me for the night. I didn't notice anyone around my apartment at all, but that was why they were so good at their jobs. I did pick up smatterings of conversation in the morning, though, as well as someone resentfully muttering "golden boy" in my general direction. No matter where I looked, I couldn't make out the source of the voice. Some Hounds were just that sneaky.

I told Romira as much. "She said she'd have some people keep watch over me."

She cleared her throat. "She wasn't any more

specific than that?" I wasn't sure if it was just the light in the break room, but it sort of looked like she was reddening.

Then it dawned on me. "Wait. She asked you to watch me, too?"

Romira smiled wolfishly. I felt my ears burning. What was I doing the night before? Did Thea regularly have me monitored? As if to allay my doubts, Romira put her hand on mine.

"No, I didn't watch you shower. And no, this isn't a habit. She was worried about you, so she called me and asked me to keep watch. It's never very specific when I see things anyway. I just have this general idea of where you are, and whether or not you're safe, same as how I found your body – I mean, when I found you in the morgue. I don't actually see you physically, just your energy signature." She trailed her eyes up and down my body, a smile lingering on her lips. "Which is a shame."

My ears were on fire. "You stop that," I said, chuckling, embarrassed, but okay, maybe flattered by the attention. "But thanks for watching over me."

Romira held my gaze a little too long for comfort. "My pleasure," she said, her words thick with exaggerated huskiness. I forced myself to laugh, my voice tinged with nervousness. She shoved a cup of coffee in my hands – she was so good at playing this game that I hadn't even noticed she was fixing me one – and started shooing me out of the kitchenette. "You come back and visit when you're all settled. And show me this room of yours when you're ready. Now I'm all curious about what the HQ dorms look like."

"You'll be the first to know," I said, winking.

Romira tossed her hair and winked back. I knew it was a harmless gesture on her part, but it still had my stomach puddling on the floor.

As if I even knew where my room was located. Who knew they even had residential suites in the Lorica? The place was full of surprises. But I hadn't made it six feet out of the kitchenette when I bumped into Thea herself. I held onto my coffee like it was a cup full of hot lava, carefully eyeing the perennial whiteness of her pantsuit, aware that I was already on her bad side.

But if Thea was annoyed with me, it didn't show, or she was making a fine effort of concealing it. "Graves," she said, nodding in greeting, the way she always did in the morning. "Good to see you in one piece. Have you set up in your new quarters yet?"

"Not just," I said, shaking my head. "I'm not even sure where to look."

Thea cocked her head. "Walk with me. I'm pretty sure they emailed me the location earlier."

I followed her in silence, duffle bag in hand, feeling for all the world like a kid on the verge of receiving his punishment. Was this really all so necessary? I'd survived the night, after all.

Couldn't they just, I don't know, put me under surveillance?

But then the thought of the Lorica expending extra Hounds and Eyes made that idea more and more ridiculous the closer we got to Thea's office. Any solid basis I might have had for making a compelling argument against moving into HQ started to crumble.

Thea swung her office door open with one hand and went straight to her computer – stark white and pristine, just like the rest of her office. She jiggled her mouse, tapped at her keyboard, then nodded.

"There it is. Far end of the east wing, room 17B."

My confusion must have shown, because I mostly just stood there and blinked. "Huh. Didn't even know there was a 17B." I scratched the back of my neck. "Come to think of it, I didn't know the Lorica made room for people to even live here in the first place."

Thea shrugged. "The Lorica – and by that I mean the building itself – makes allowances for whatever we need. Sometimes people need extra protection, or we need to put them under surveillance. Somehow the Lorica makes room for that."

I wondered if I was being brought in merely for protection, or for surveillance as well. I decided it was best not to ask. But that didn't mean that the stupid side of me was done talking or thinking. Without considering it, I blurted out my earlier thoughts.

"But is this even necessary? I mean, those guys were scared off. I'm pretty sure they're not coming back for me, not that they even know where to look."

The atmosphere in her office seemed to shiver, like the serenity of it had been interrupted. Remember when I said that the offices were reflections of their occupants' inner selves? I didn't realize I was so very correct. Thea's office darkened, just slightly so, enough to match the disapproving look on her face, and the sunlight streaming in through the windows felt that much harsher.

"This is the better option, Dustin." Thea's jewelry clicked against her desk as she lay her palms flat against it. "You'll be safer here."

I scratched at the bridge of my nose, fully aware that I should stop probing and resisting, but I just couldn't shut up. "Why would they even want me?"

The room seemed to darken just that little bit more. "Oh, I don't know, Dustin. Maybe because you found the bodies? You were somewhere you weren't supposed to be. And have you considered the possibility that those men might have something to do with the night you were murdered? The Black Hand, remember? How can you be so brazen about this?"

I think I might have tuned the rest of it out,

not for want of quiet, but because this was all stuff I'd heard and told myself before. I bit my lip and alternated between staring at the ground and mournfully up into Thea's face as she gave me the tongue-lashing of a lifetime. It was a full few minutes before she stopped, and by then her cheeks were rosier from the effort, and, far likelier, the irritation.

"I'm sorry," I said, unsure of what else to say.

Thea sighed, like a long-suffering mother. "Don't apologize. Just promise you won't do anything silly on your own from now on." She shook her head and drummed her fingers against her desk. "Just stick to the inside of the Lorica for now. This isn't a permanent thing, Dustin, don't worry. And you'll be allowed supervised time out if you feel like going somewhere. But for now, just keep a low profile, okay?"

I nodded. I could tell from her eyes and her tone that this was all out of concern. Thea was just looking out for me, after all, and I was being the stubborn knucklehead who kept defying her. I almost found myself saying "I'll be good," but caught myself in time.

"I'll go move into my bunk, then."

That got a small laugh out of her, at least. "Okay, you go do that. I'll check in on you later. We might have something for you to do around here after all." I nodded, then quietly let myself out of her office.

I was right about 17B, as it turned out. No one

had heard of it, at least none of the regulars I'd asked, and it was further off into the east wing than I'd ever ventured. It gave new meaning to what Thea was saying about the Lorica providing for its own, almost as if the building had a sentience to it, accommodating me in this new section that had seemingly been carved out of empty space.

It wasn't exactly difficult to find the room, either. I'd only taken a few steps in the general direction of my new quarters when I noticed the designs in the carpet shifting, changing shape. The carpet was unfurling a new pattern made completely out of pulsing red and blue arrows, all pointing towards the east wing.

I decided early on that sometimes it was best not to question how these things worked, though I admit I had some reservations about sleeping there. I mean, if the building could create a new room out of thin air, who was to say that it couldn't reclaim that space whenever it wanted?

But quite a lot of my doubts dissolved just as soon as I opened the door to 17B. It was cozy, actually, and warm, and going by decor alone it was much better than my own apartment by leaps and bounds. Everything on the inside was white – a by-product of the fact that it was Thea who had requisitioned the space – but that was fine by me. I thought it would be nice to live in a room that didn't have peeling paint or carpeting curling up in the corners for once.

All the room had were a couple of chairs and a table, a closet, and a comfy-looking bed, all in fetching shades of Thea's signature ivory. I started to unpack on the bed, feeling extra sensitive about spilling any of my toiletries on the pristine perfection of the sheets, when I had a keen sense that something was, I don't know, shifting, somehow. I turned around, only to find that the sparse furniture and closet had lost their gleaming whiteness, now exhibiting a wooden finish instead.

Huh. This was more my speed. Thea wasn't kidding. The room – or the part of the Lorica that was designated as my room – was adjusting to me, and I watched with bemusement as the walls slid lazily into a pale gray, the color of a midday storm.

I turned back to the bed, ready to unpack in this decidedly more comfortable environment, and tried not to be too pleased with myself when the bed frame morphed from a white-painted metal to a much homier wooden design, the sheets dyeing themselves before my very eyes from shocking white to a deep midnight blue, finished with tiny speckles that made the bed look like a field of stars. Awesome.

I put away my stuff, hanging what clothes I had in the closet, then went to the bathroom to freshen up. Sure, I'd gotten some sleep the night before, a little to ease the exhaustion from those consecutive work days, but it didn't quite feel like enough. I figured splashing some cold water on my face would help.

Even as I stepped into the blinding white of the bathroom it took on the same midnight blue as my bedsheets, making the shower stall and the tiles gleam like deep sapphires. Briefly I wondered how much it would cost to actually do up my place to look like this. The whole living at HQ thing might not be so bad, I figured, twisting the faucet.

Ice-cold water did the trick to help keep me standing on my feet, but I knew I'd have to down another cup of coffee before long. I turned off the faucet then rubbed at my eyes long enough to look in the mirror, then nearly jumped when I saw a different face staring back at me.

"Bastion. Jesus. You trying to kill me?"

He was standing behind me, staring back through the mirror in what was supposed to look like genuine surprise, but I knew him well enough. The bastard had crept up on me just to freak me out.

Bastion shrugged, the smile creeping across his lips just equal parts friendly and condescending. "What, hey. I was just dropping by to say hello. Why are you so jumpy all of a sudden?"

Maybe, I thought, it was because of all the bizarre surprises I'd had over the course of just a few days. Harrowing encounters with faces thrust up against mine, for example, like that episode with Arachne where I thought she was going to eat my face off shortly before she kissed me, or that run-in with the vampire who clearly had no concept of personal space. But I said none of those things and just frowned at him in the mirror.

"Can I help you, Brandt? Kind of busy here."

Bastion snorted. "Washing your face?"

"Yes, busy washing my face. What do you want, anyway? Can't a guy get a little bathroom time on his own around here?"

Bastion folded his arms. "I guess not. You've got to admit, this is all pretty – unorthodox. And I'm not here stalking you. You think I make a habit of exploring every new place that pops up in HQ?"

He had a point. I was pretty sure that nobody apart from Thea and admin knew about 17B. Which meant –

"Thea sent you?"

Bastion shrugged. "For whatever reason. Said to wait for her here."

I had an immediate sinking feeling. That my earlier encounter with Thea had involved such a severe haranguing made the prospect of seeing her again so soon less than pleasurable. I wiped irritably at my forehead with the back of my sleeve.

"Don't do that," Bastion said, unfolding his arms, almost reaching out with a hand to stop me. "Here." He tossed me a towel from the pile on my bed.

"Um. Thanks." I rubbed at my face, eyeing him warily.

"No, no. You should dab. Just, like, pat at your face. Gives you wrinkles otherwise, if you're too harsh with your skin."

"Wow. Okay. Wasn't expecting beauty tips from you, but here we are." I patted at my skin as he watched, his expression a little too vigilant. "You do this yourself?"

Bastion nodded, his face stern, serious. "Keeps me pretty."

I laughed. This might have been the longest we'd been in the same space without wanting to kill each other. But then a voice drifted in from the doorway, and I felt relief in knowing that the pressure of discovering whether I could actually be friends with Bastion was off.

"This isn't so bad," Prudence said, walking in with her arms folded, appraising the room.

"Yeah?" I said, grinning. I panicked, briefly, wondering if I had left any of my underwear on my bed. Quick check: I was clear. I'd packed it all in the closet. "You like what I've done with the place?"

Bastion grunted. "I mean it hardly took any effort."

I tutted and cocked my head. "You had to ruin it, Brandt. And you and I were getting along so well, too."

"Play nice, boys."

Thea's voice flooded the room with its authority, and both Bastion and Prudence's spines went straighter just as soon as she walked in. It was a reminder that even in the arcane underground, everyone knew that you were supposed to look and be your sharpest when your boss was sniffing around.

"That's what I keep telling them," Prudence said. I tried to get her attention, to give her a betrayed look, but I could tell she was avoiding my gaze.

"They'll learn to get along with each other soon enough," Thea said.

Ominous. Bastion's breathing hitched. I broke the silence, directing my question at Thea.

"Is. Is there some reason the two of them are here?"

I could swear her face almost cracked from the effort of trying not to smile. "Because Leung and Brandt are your bodyguards now."

Prudence seemed unsurprised, but Bastion and I must have cried out in protest at precisely the same time.

Bastion piled more kindling on the fire, thrusting an accusing finger in my face. "What makes him so damn important, anyway?"

"Bastion. Shush." Thea turned to me. "Dustin, I've told you enough times. It isn't safe for you to be out there on your own anymore. But just because there's all this going down right now, doesn't mean that your training has to stop. We need all the information we can get, and I trust you enough to initiate your own communion now."

The memory of Arachne's domicile, sickly green and venomous, stuck at my throat. "You mean I'm going to talk to an entity?"

"As the initiator, yes, on your own. Prudence and Bastion will accompany you, but only as your protectors. You will perform the ritual to access the domicile yourself, and you will attempt to curry the entity's favor." She raised her head just the fraction of an inch higher, as if slightly proud.

"You did so well the last time that I'm confident you'll do just as well this go around. If you get more information about the murders, so much the better. And if you somehow finagle a contract out of this, well, that would be the very best outcome. It can't hurt for you to find some way to defend yourself."

For what felt like the third time, Bastion scoffed.

"Brandt," Prudence shot out. "Please." She looked to me, as if sensing my confusion. "A contract represents what an entity might do for you. Think of it as a gift, whether it's information, or a favor. Even power."

My spine tingled. "Power?"

Thea nodded. "We all have limits to the magic we can exhaust from our bodies and our surroundings, but an entity – especially a strong one – might grant you the ability to dip into their well, so to speak."

"It's like hooking yourself up to a generator," Bastion said. "One that doesn't quit."

"Holy crap." That was what happened the night the vampire chased me. I'd used my magic so much that my tank was running on empty. My head buzzed at the prospect of a contract.

"Exactly," Thea said. "And it's crucial that you wrap this all up because the clock is ticking. There's been another murder."

Bastion frowned. I gaped. Prudence didn't flinch at all. She already knew, on top of things as she always was.

"Lei Kung," Prudence said. "A thunder god, from the Chinese pantheon. Not quite as known or as influential as the big wigs like Thor or Zeus, but his destruction will still have its impact."

"Same circumstances," Thea said. "Coaxed out of the protection of his realm and slain in our world. Time will tell how long it'll take for his absence to warp this reality."

As if on cue, a massive peal of thunder rocked the air outside of HQ. The lights flickered. I exchanged a wary glance with Bastion, then turned back to Thea, mouth dry.

"Sooner than we thought, apparently," she said. "Best get a move on. Get more information, or seal a contract. Just do something."

"I'll do my best," I croaked. "But who are we talking to this time?"

"Someone a little more fickle, and I dare say a

little more esoteric than our friend Arachne. This one has a tendency to speak in puzzles, and I think it's safe to say that she's remarkably more dangerous, which is why your charisma will be infinitely important in sweetening your communion."

"Dangerous?" I said, not meaning to groan, but fully doing so anyway. I looked to both Prudence and Bastion for a reaction, but if they were fearful or uncomfortable at all with what we were being tasked to do, they didn't show it.

"Dangerous, yes," Thea said. "Comes with the territory. After all, it's not every day you'll be tasked to commune with an actual goddess of magic."

Chapter 10

The club was called Temple, and it was packed with beautiful people come to worship and adore each other, or the DJ, or the lure of a watery cocktail. Temple vibrated, both from the music and the sudden thunderstorm raging outside. I could feel the music in my throat, trying to punch its way into, or out of my body. It was hard to tell.

It was synth wave disco industrial baby killer night, or some other string of words I probably got in the wrong order. Don't get me wrong, I love me some electronic music, but tonight the DJ was spinning something that sounded like a lawnmower trying to eat another lawnmower.

I looked over at Prudence, who clearly felt very much the same way. Her face was wrinkled up as we maneuvered our way through the crowd, trying to push through the swell of people to reach the bar at the far end of the establishment.

Who knew why they wanted a packed dance floor up front, but if the plan was to attract more business by showing that they had a full house of writhing supermodels grinding it out just by the entrance, then they did it right.

Prudence's mood was darkening with every unintentional jostle a dancer inflicted on her, and I knew her fists were balled up so tightly that her fingernails were digging into her skin. Bastion, on the other hand, was clearly loving it, and that just made me hate him a little bit more.

He was dancing, not at all badly, I noted, as we wove our way through the throng. Here and there he would lean in and whisper something in someone's ear, though how he managed to get anything through over the pounding dance music was anyone's guess. But it got the intended reaction anyway.

The women he whispered to threw him intrigued glances as he half-sauntered, half-ground his way across the dance floor. Once I saw him touch a girl lightly on the forearm, the friendly grin on his face returned with batted eyelashes and a simper. I thought we were there for work, but apparently we'd thrust Bastion directly into his element, and he was thoroughly enjoying every second of it.

We made it to the far end of the club, close enough to the bar that shouting at the top of our lungs would let us understand each other again. It was at that point that Prudence had obviously had enough, and she dragged Bastion bodily away from the last girl he had made contact with, cuffing him by the collar.

The girl locked eyes with Prudence, then thought better of a confrontation. Bastion, to my surprise, took his separation in good humor and merely adjusted his leather jacket. I didn't need to hear to understand what he was saying. I could make it out from the way he held up his hands and shrugged, head cocked to the side.

"Aww, come on, Prue. There's plenty for everybody."

Through the multicolored strobe lights of the club, I could still see Prudence's cheeks going an angry red. She had to work with this guy on a regular, mind you. How she managed to stop herself from punching him in the teeth every five minutes was anybody's guess.

I followed as she dragged him to the bar, which may as well have been a parade float. Three bartenders worked the semi-circular counter, allowing them to sling drinks to everyone within a hundred and eighty degrees. It was a neon behemoth, done up in the hot pinks and electric blues that were all the rage in the eighties, and that seemed to be coming back for some temporary renaissance. Hell, it was six times bigger than the DJ's booth. I kind of felt bad for him, but I guess Temple really liked making money.

"So what exactly are we doing here again?" I yelled to no one in particular.

"Gathering information," Prudence yelled back. "We need to find the entity's gateway." Mercifully, she stopped moving towards the bar, saving me the indignity of screaming myself hoarse.

But I had to cup my hands over my mouth to get my point across anyway. "Don't we just check a map for that?"

Bastion's guffawing carried over the relentless boom-boom of the club's speakers. It was like a dog whistle, and I was pretty certain that even after we had left Temple, hours after my eardrums had been blown out, I'd still be able to hear nothing except the exact infuriating frequency of his laughter.

He made gestures with his hands, subtle ones that could have looked like someone motioning as he spoke, his lips moving the whole time. Not that a casual observer would have been able to tell by Temple's flashing interiors, but his fingers left strands of white light as he worked. He ended the sequence by running his hand through his hair – because even when casting a spell, Sebastion Brandt could still be kind of a douche.

A faint tingling sheared through the air. The noise around us seemed duller, the pulsing beat of the club muted, and when he spoke, I could almost hear him in my ear.

"Honestly, Graves," he said, grinning that self-satisfied grin. "It's like you never pay attention, even when your mom's talking."

I knew he was talking about Thea, but somehow Bastion's schoolyard bully jab of bringing up my mother – even though he had no way of knowing she was dead – stung more than it should have. I said nothing.

"She wasn't just saying things out loud when she said the entity was fickle," he continued. "That applies for its personality, sure, and how we're supposed to deal with it, but the entity's gateway is fickle as well."

I looked around us, wondering why he was being so blase about relaying this information when I realized that whatever spell he cast had made it so that only we could hear each other. Outside our little circle everyone was still yelling to make themselves heard, especially the ever-replenishing rush of people putting in their orders at the bar.

"So who are we supposed to talk to?" I waved at the bartenders, two men and one woman, all busy pouring drinks and fielding orders. "Doubt we can even get their attention long enough to grab a beer."

Bastion rolled his eyes. "No, dum-dum. Look closer."

"Honestly, Bastion." Prudence clapped me on the back and nudged her head towards the bar. "Part of your training is to learn to perceive things that are out of the ordinary. That'll help you on the field as much as it will help in everyday life now that you've seen bits of the underground. You have to learn to notice what's different, to pick things out."

"Okay," I said, looking along the bar. "I'm not sure I see any – wait."

And there she was, camouflaged among the revelers before Prudence told me to look, but suddenly sticking out to me plain as day. There were stools along the bar, perfect for anyone who didn't feel up to dancing or wrestling with the throng to get one of the very few booths or tables strewn about the club.

All the stools were taken, but one occupant stood out more than the rest. Her hair was dark, but it shone with the color of a sun dying on the horizon, brassy, like black silk flecked with gold. Her lips were a deep red, her eyes like obsidian, her skin dusky and deep.

Yet as striking as the woman was, what I found more remarkable was the collection of glasses around her, drinks drained of just enough liquid to leave clues to their former existence, all these puddles of color thinning with melting ice. As I watched, more cocktails appeared, delivered by men with hollow eyes who only passed long enough to place a glass by her side, then left again.

The bartenders, I noticed, were giving her a wide berth, hence the growing stacks of glasses.

Something was amiss here, and I wasn't sure I wanted to find out what it was. Then the woman turned and fixed me with her gaze.

My breath caught in my throat. With her smoldering eyes, her hair like dark fire, her perfect skin, she was unmistakeably beautiful, but in a way that was so unearthly, supernatural. It reminded me of the pale man. I shuddered, and I hoped she didn't see.

I drew up to Prudence as subtly as I could. "Is – is that another vampire?"

"Close," Prudence said, looking off and away, as if to hide her face from the woman. Her lip was upturned in distaste. "Succubus."

I couldn't help it. My jaw dropped open. "What? As in a soul-sucking demon? That kind of succubus?" Honestly, I thought to myself, wincing. What other kind was there?

She nudged me in the ribs. "Cool it. No one can really hear us from outside the bubble Bastion cast, but she can still read your lips. But yes. As to whether that's worse than a vampire, you decide."

Bastion draped his arm heavily across my shoulder and pulled me in. I cringed at the proximity, and at the choking scent of his body spray.

"Aww. Is Dusty afraid of the pretty lady?"

"Shut up. I'm not afraid. Just – I have reason to be wary given recent events, okay?"

"It's not like anyone hurt you," Bastion said.

"Just be polite, play nice, and Layla will tell us what we need. She's harmless." There was a pause. "Well, mostly."

"Question," I said, carefully eyeing the woman, and wearing the politest smile I could muster. Her expression remained unchanged, and her gaze was still trained on me. "Don't they have their own domiciles? Succubi, vampires. Aren't they entities, too?"

"Well," Prudence said, rubbing her chin. "In a way. It's the smart, resourceful ones who make their own domiciles. That's like spiritual real estate, their place of power. Think of it like building a business. You'd be surprised how powerful these things can grow. Look at Arachne. She's not even a god. Any entity can work hard enough and create their own base of operations. It's a matter of time and effort."

"God bless America," Bastion said.

"Hush. Anyway. You try going into an entity's domicile to stir up trouble, you'll end up dead real quick. And I'm pretty sure they're unkillable in their own home realms. They'll just regenerate after a time. The rest of them are tied to our plane. Since they're tethered here, death is death. The free-running ones are more vulnerable. But long story short: yes, she's still totally dangerous."

The woman with the flaming hair finally shifted, her smile friendlier. She blinked, just the once, and it sent something fluttering down my spine. Was it demon magic, or her eldritch beauty? Did it really matter?

"So you're saying there's more of these beings running around. More vampires and succubuses. Succubi?"

Prudence nodded. "They behave, mostly, because you've got forces like the Lorica to keep things in order. But's it's not just them, of course. You've got demons, angels, ifrits, fae." Her nose wrinkled up. "Gotta watch out for those fae."

"Great," I groaned, breaking eye contact with the succubus. "More things that can kill us dead."

Bastion shrugged, making me newly aware of how he was still in my space, like a leech. "Pretty much."

I wriggled out of his grasp. "Let's just get this over with."

"Agreed," Prudence said, nodding.

She led us to the bar, striding confidently and, I thought, maybe a little threateningly. The succubus – Layla, that was her name – watched us from behind a wisp of her hair, her hand in her chin, her lips curved in a languorous smile. Something rippled in the air around us as we approached, the effect of her being allowed into the bubble of silence that Bastion had crafted. Layla's smile grew at that, as if she sensed the veil of magic around her. Her gaze flitted from me, to Prudence, then came to rest on Bastion's face.

"You never called me," she cooed.

Her voice was like a breeze blowing across a

still desert: tranquil, soothing, yet deep, and somehow vast. I couldn't place her accent, and I couldn't tell if that was because it shifted in places, or because it seemed to be a blend of sounds and slurs from across continents. Where was she from?

But truthfully what really poked at me was how old she was. Were succubi like vampires? She might have been in the hundreds, as if I had any way of telling. On some level I suspected that seniority worked the same way for entities as they did with mages and their ages: the older they were, the more powerful. But I didn't dare ask. I had a feeling she wouldn't at all appreciate me prying.

Bastion leaned on the bar with one elbow, his smile brighter than all the lights in the vicinity. I could tell that he was arranging his posture, his face, even the timbre of his voice to be as appealing as humanly possible, clearly intent on charming the succubus. I'm not gonna lie, I was secretly taking notes in my head. I never pass up an opportunity to learn something new.

"Layla, you're a beautiful, soul-sucking nether demon. I'm a beautiful, soul-sucking loser. We're too similar. It'd never work out."

Prudence's spine seemed to stiffen at that. Mine too, frankly. It was some pretty daring shit to say to what could very well have been a centuries-old demon. But Layla only threw her head back and laughed, the sound of it like little brass bells.

"You are too right, Sebastion. So I hope you have brought me something entertaining in your stead." She took the barest fraction of a second to cast her eyes up and down Prudence's body, just long enough to show her disinterest. "This one, I already know. She is no fun."

Prudence grunted. "It's nice to see you too, Layla."

The demon shifted in her seat, leaning her chin into her hand again, this coquettish pose that made me believe she was just some young girl looking to have fun in a club, and not an ancient fiend from somewhere sandy and blasted with heat.

I wondered how many men and women she had seduced from her throne at Temple's bar, and as she smiled to show two rows of perfect teeth it dawned on me that she wasn't hanging out for free drinks. Layla was here for a different kind of sustenance. I swallowed, hard, and took the greatest care not to show that anything was amiss.

"Now this one," she said. "This one intrigues me." Maybe one of the strobes hit her just then, or maybe it was the ambient glow of the bar's many neon lights, but her eyes brightened as they locked with mine, and my heart stuttered for just the briefest moment. Get it together, I told myself. This is what she's made for, to break you apart, then crack you open so she can feed. As if sensing my thoughts, her lips parted wider and she laughed.

"Why are you so nervous? I'm not going to eat you." Which would have been a far more innocuous statement if her tongue hadn't picked that exact moment to run across the edge of her teeth. It only made me jumpier. "Come closer," she said.

Bastion slid away from her slowly, making space for me at the counter. The hardness in his eyes and the tightness in his lips said it all: this is the job, and you're here to do it. You'd have to rip off my fingernails to get me to admit it, but in that moment Bastion gave me just the encouragement I needed to get things done. I straightened my back, and maybe broadened my shoulders a bit. I knew I could do it.

"I'm not nervous," I said, easing my forearm onto the counter, wearing an easy smile. "Just entranced, maybe. You're the prettiest thing around here, after all."

From behind me, I heard Bastion's intake of breath. Maybe he was laughing, or maybe it was actually a snort of approval. Didn't matter. From a little further off I heard Prudence snort, too. That I interpreted with zero trouble.

"Goodness," Layla said, her hand hovering over her mouth. "If this one isn't forward! I quite like you, new boy."

"First month on the job, ma'am," I said, tipping an imaginary hat. "Dustin Graves, at your service."

Layla placed a hand on the counter, fingers drumming lazily at the plexiglass. Her nails were painted a deep red to match her lips, like drops of blood at the end of each finger.

"Dustin," she said, leaning forward, the unsubtle cut of her dress threatening to give me a closer view of her admittedly generous bosoms. Focus, I told myself. "You're charming, I confess, but I bet you say that to all the demons."

"That's quite impossible, Layla." I grinned again. "You're my first, after all."

The demon flushed, then squealed in delight, hiding her lips behind one delicate hand. This was starting to remind me of my time with Arachne. Gotta stay vigilant, I told myself. I looked over my shoulder to see if Bastion had anything to say about how I was doing, but he was gazing out into the crowd of dancers, his attention already wandering.

Prudence was doing the same – rather, alternating between examining her nails and swiping at her phone – but I got the sense that both were putting on airs and were still listening intently to everything that was going on with Layla.

"Buy you a drink?" I said. That much I remembered from Thea, that these encounters with the entities were all transactions, and something needed to be traded, especially for something as valuable as information. I could only hope that a cocktail would be all I needed.

"Brandy Alexander," Layla said, never taking her eyes off me. I peeled a couple of bills out of my wallet, catching the attention of one of the bartenders.

"Keep the change," I said, winking at Layla and thickening my voice with braggadocio. She squirmed in her seat. The bartender glanced between us. He shook his head, then took off to fill the order.

"Now Layla." I clasped my hands in front of me, lacing my fingers and resting them on the counter. "As pleasant as this is, I do have to admit that we need something from you."

She sighed, twirling a lock of her hair around one finger. "That's all you Lorica boys ever want. And what does poor Layla ever get?"

I cocked one shoulder. "Lots of compliments, and cocktails? Not a bad deal, I should say."

Layla lowered her gaze. "Naughty. But correct." She spread her fingers across the counter, then lifted her nose, her demeanor somber, serious. I was more aware than ever of the silence around us. "Tell me what you need."

"Gateway," I said, forcing myself not to react to her sudden chill. "We need to find Hecate."

Her eyes widened, and she burst into a huff. "Hah! Hecate? In these conditions? You're better off talking to a fortune teller." She slipped one hand into her clutch, sifting through its contents. "I've got my psychic's number right here. The woman's certifiably insane and gets nothing right, I just like listening."

I cleared my throat and tightened the clasping of my fingers. "We'd prefer if you could tell us where her portal is tethered. We really need to speak with her."

Layla stopped shuffling through her purse, setting it back down on the counter. Her eyes squinted in suspicion. "So what you're telling me is that you need information – so you can seek her out for more information."

"I. Uh. Yes."

Layla threw one hand up and waved it dismissively. "I'll never understand you humans. Sometimes you just have to take action, you know? Back in the day, if we had a problem, we did something." She groped for thin air, then clenched her hand into a fist, fingernails gleaming like sharpened rubies. "Reach into someone's chest, rip their heart out. Done." She dusted her hands off. "No drama. Efficient."

I wondered how much of that was true and did my best not to stammer. "We can't take action without knowing who's at fault, though. It's about the murder of the god Resheph, if you've heard of it."

She nodded, her eyes looking distant. "I have, actually. I knew some of the gods from his pantheon, nice people. Didn't know him personally, but it's a damn shame." Her eyes refocused on mine, but the warmth was still missing, all business now. "Right. So you already know that Hecate's gateway shifts, correct? It's only sensible. She's trying to keep herself safe. Who knows where the murderer will pounce next?"

I nodded along. The shifting tether was a practical safeguard, well and good, but it did make tracking down our contact a bigger pain in the ass.

"So what you're really asking for is the exact location of Hecate's tether. Where it is at this very moment." Layla's eyes narrowed, and the shadow of a smile crept back to her lips. "That's going to cost you more than a Brandy Alexander."

"Oh, come on now, Layla," Bastion's voice cooed from just past my ear. Had his head been poked into the conversation the whole time?

She held up a hand. "Bastion. Shush. This is between me and the new boy." She tilted her head, her smile now fully returned. "What do you say, Mr. Graves? All it takes is one kiss."

Chapter 11

Bastion's fingers dug into my shoulder, stabbing right through my jacket. His whispers were urgent. "Bro, don't do it, bro."

I grimaced. We needed Layla, I was sure of it. Why would we have come all this way if that wasn't the case? I turned my head slightly, careful not to let Layla see or hear me speak. "It's not like we have a choice, Bastion."

Out of the corner of my eye I caught Prudence frowning in our general direction. Her face said it all. She obviously didn't approve of what was about to happen, but it needed to be done. I sighed. All in a day's work.

I mustered my courage, and whatever was left of my good graces, and turned to Layla with a neutral expression. "Okay," I said. "One kiss."

She didn't reply, but her smile said it all.

"Is it – " I began. "Will it hurt?"

Layla pushed a lock of hair out of her face, the apples of her cheeks going rosier with every passing moment. "Only a little." She raised her chin, exposing part of her throat, as if she was trying to get me to mirror her and offer my own vulnerability. "Whatever I take from you will return over time. Like blood. Your body will always make more."

Maybe it was the dazzle of colored lights that did it, but I didn't catch Layla closing the distance between us. The counter, the bar, the club disappeared when she pressed her lips against mine. They were warm, and only a little wet, lined with something sweet that had just come out of a glass. I steadied myself as she leaned in, her mouth hungry, and maybe it stung a little when I remembered that she wasn't into me as much as she wanted to devour a part of my soul.

Her tongue moved against mine, and I couldn't stop the moan that left my mouth and echoed its way into the tunnel of our locked bodies. From somewhere behind me I was vaguely aware of Bastion exhaling in something that sounded like a low whistle. Any lingering traces of liquor on Layla's lips had vanished, and other tastes and impossible sensations worked their way across my tongue: incense, earth, the scent and flavor of rose petals.

Then her nails dug into my back.

I tried to tear myself away as something inside of Layla's mouth forced itself into my body. Not anything physical, but a sensation of something slithering down my throat, reaching and probing inside of me, then gripping at whatever it had found within my core. Whatever it was dug its way into me, a slender hand with its dozens upon dozens of fingers. Then it squeezed.

I cried out, but Layla's lips were locked like iron against mine, the size and shape of her body belying the horrific strength behind her arms. My eyes flew open, and maybe she didn't look any different, but I finally saw her for the voracious demon she was, latched onto my mouth and onto my soul like a lamprey. I saw Prudence approaching, her face like thunder. Against my mouth, I felt the succubus smiling.

And just as suddenly as the pain had shot through my body, as she had grabbed me to kiss – to feed – Layla shoved me away. Not with the playful push of a temptress concluding her seduction, either, but like someone burned. Her breathing was hoarse as our mouths came apart, her eyebrows creased in fury. She spat and wiped at her lips, stabbing one finger at me, the blood drop of her nail glinting in accusation.

"Poison." She pointed at Prudence, then at Bastion in turn. "You're trying to poison me." She hissed, her teeth gleaming. They were nowhere near as sharp as the vampire's, but it still made me take a step back.

Prudence stepped in, elbowing me out of the way. "We don't know what you're talking about, demon. We filled our end of the bargain. You took part of his soul. Now give us what we need."

The bartender showed up just then, gingerly placing Layla's Brandy Alexander on the counter, then looking between us, deciding whether to call on one of the club's many bouncers. I couldn't be sure if it was a glare from Layla or Prudence that did it, but he lifted his hands in placation and backed away, slowly.

Layla brought the glass to her lips and drained the cocktail in one gulp. It might have been my imagination but I swear her mouth went wider then, like a snake with its jaw unhinged. I still didn't know enough about demons to tell if I was just seeing things, but it wasn't the time to ask. And poison? She picked up a napkin and dabbed at her lips, the anger mostly gone from her face, but her eyes still cold, murderous.

"Maybe it wasn't deliberate," she said. "But this one is different. There's a darkness inside him. His soul is tainted."

Bastion slung his arm over my shoulder and chuckled throatily. "Didn't need to kiss him to know that, Layla."

I shrugged him off and puckered my lips, blowing a mock kiss the way he did to me just the other day. "Night's still young, sweet cheeks. Never too late to find out." Bastion slunk away, his neck turning a subtle shade of red. I guess he hadn't expected me to fight back. Hah. Small victories.

Layla snapped her fingers, summoning another bartender. I wasn't sure if I should have been offended at how she was draining even the remains of her used-up cocktails, like kissing me had been the most disgusting experience.

"Nothing personal, new boy. It's just – there's something wrong with you." Her eyes narrowed, then flitted towards Prudence. "The deal's off."

This time it wasn't the strobe lights. There was definitely a flash of blue luminescence as Prudence clenched her right fist. I wasn't sure if it was meant to be an intentional threat, but Layla shifted visibly in her seat.

"Like hell it is," Prudence growled. "You agreed to provide information in exchange for a kiss. A kiss that claimed part of a human soul, you scum-sucking hell beast."

Layla bared her teeth and hissed, a feral display that would have made me jump back, but Prudence held her ground.

"An arcane soul too, may I remind you. I know your kind, succubus. You demons may have your own ways of doing things, but you hold to your word." Prudence folded her arms across her chest, raising her chin triumphantly. "An agreement is an agreement."

Layla slammed her fist on the counter. Empty glasses jiggled and clinked at the impact. I steeled myself and didn't dare show my reaction when I noticed the hairline cracks spidering from the point where her punch had landed.

"Back alley of the Phat Pharm. There's a dead pigeon on the asphalt, by a dumpster. The pigeon is the locus. Cast your circle there. Now leave me alone." She turned to the bar again, pounding her open hand against the counter. "Whiskey sour. And can you make sure it gets to me some time this decade?"

Layla threw me one last accusing look, then turned away, and I knew we were dismissed. Without a word, Prudence grabbed me by the forearm and tugged me out of the club, with Bastion following along behind us.

I thought I'd done something wrong somehow. We got out on the street, the wet sidewalk now the only sign that a freak thunderstorm had passed through. Prudence clapped me on the back, her expression something almost approaching pride.

"You did good in there. Didn't flinch when she asked to take a bite out of you." She looked to Bastion expectantly. I thought she was going to start tapping her foot.

Bastion turned up his lip and stuck his hands deep into his jacket pockets, pretending to be disinterested as he looked up, then down the street. "Yeah," he mumbled grudgingly. "Took one for the team. Good job, I guess."

I grinned. I didn't have a lot of opportunities

to gloat right in Bastion's face, so I took my shot. "Hey," I said, spreading my arms out. "You just have to believe in me. You just – you just have to trust in Dustin."

Prudence snorted. Bastion groaned.

Still, what the succubus said lingered like a bad smell. "That taint Layla was talking about, though. The darkness inside me? What did she mean?"

"Beats me. Consider yourself lucky she didn't latch on for much longer." Prudence shrugged, tapped at something on her phone, then took off down the sidewalk, boot heels clicking at the rain-slicked pavement.

"Yo," Bastion called out. "What's the hurry?" I thought much the same as I tried to match her stride.

"Twenty-four-hour supermarket this way," Prudence said, barely missing a beat. "We have the tether's location, but we still need to shop for reagents. To open the gateway, remember?"

Bastion smoothed his hair back, adjusting his jacket as he caught up. "Relax. How hard can it be to crack the entity's domicile?"

Prudence brought her phone closer to her face as she walked, her expression stony in the pale blue glow. "For Hecate? Some honey." She grimaced. "And a black lamb." Her features darkened further. "And maybe a dog."

Bastion stopped in his tracks, but when he noticed Prudence was still walking, made double time to catch up again.

"Wait, you're kidding, right? Not a doggie." There was a quality to his voice that I'd rarely ever heard, something with an edge of a desperate whine to it. His tone kept thinning as he talked. "Prue? Not a puppy. Right?"

Prudence just kept walking.

Chapter 12

"I can't believe she's keeping us in suspense like this," Bastion mumbled. His mouth was pushed into the collar of his leather jacket, his voice muffled. Couldn't blame him, it was cold in the alley. "She's doing this on purpose, I bet."

I shrugged and shook my head. "She wanted us to scout ahead and make sure the pigeon was here." I nudged the dead bird with my toe. It was rock hard, from both rigor mortis and the chill of the pavement. "Which reminds me."

I fired off a quick text message to let Prudence know we'd found the tether. She had sent us ahead to look over the pigeon and make sure that it wouldn't move again. I took that to mean that she was worried about a cat coming across it and carrying it off. I wasn't exactly sure how that would work out – what would even happen to an animal that ate an entity's tether? – but at least we'd secured the damn thing.

My skin crawled as I heard tiny paws scuttling in the dark corners of the alley. Ah. So we arrived just before the scavengers did. I kicked at the ground, scuffing my heels loudly, just to scare the rats away from the pigeon. Valero's rodents really had gone unhinged since Resheph's death. I reached for my phone, trying to distract myself from the squirming march of glistening, furry bodies ducking in and out of dumpsters.

There was already a notification on my screen. "K" was all that Prudence wrote in her text. Typical. We all knew she was efficient, almost surgically so, but I would have appreciated more information. She'd gone to do the reagent shopping herself, doubtless to get Bastion to stop whining about the puppy. I offered to go with her, but it became clear quite quickly that she meant for me to distract him while she went about collecting what we needed.

"Not a puppy," he said again.

Sorry, not distract. I think babysit would have been the right word. I sighed.

"Listen. I'm as against the idea as you are, but if that's what we need to do to get the job done – "

My words hung in the air. I couldn't say it. I had been more dedicated to my work for the Lorica than I had been to virtually anything else in my life, more than my shitty treatment of my high school education, and certainly more than any of the odd jobs I picked up after. But a dog?

Hell, a lamb, for that matter? Where was Prudence even going to find either one of those at midnight in Valero? And that wasn't even the point. I realized that part of casting the circle to enter an entity's domicile or to even attract its attention involved sacrifice. The offerings, like the fortune cookie Thea crumbled, or the drop of blood. They were necessary components for completing the ritual, for closing the circle.

But I still had my limits. "Okay. Fine. I'm with you. Are we sure about what we're doing here? I mean, a puppy."

"Stop," Bastion groaned. "But yes. It's worse with some of the others. These are ancient gods we're talking about, remember? Some of them — some of them expect more, um, exotic sacrifices."

Bumps rose everywhere on my skin, and I can tell you that it wasn't because of the cold. "Go on," I said.

He studiously avoided my gaze. "You know how it is. How it was. We don't work with those kinds of entities. It's nothing to worry about. It's just that some of the more ancient cultures, certain pantheons, they expect something bigger. Something bloodier."

"Certain pantheons. Right." I wanted to know. I needed to know if that was why I'd been killed, if I was meant to be a sacrifice for a being that, according to Thea, was worse than an entity in every way. "Certain pantheons – or the Eldest."

"Dude, shut up." Bastion bared his teeth as he shushed me, his breath hissing out of him in a puff of fog. "What are you, crazy? Who told you about that shit?"

"Thea," I said hurriedly. "Those people who killed me, what if they did it for a purpose? To commune with the Eldest?"

Bastion frowned. "That's batshit insane and you know it, Graves. You don't 'commune' with the Eldest. You make contact, you die. And that's if you're lucky." He walked up to me, uncomfortably close, his stare menacing. "You could be driven insane just from the sight of them. Or warped – I'm talking proper mutated, and turned into their plaything – just a sculpture made out of flesh and bone. And you can't move, but you see them always, your eyes unblinking. You live forever. You scream forever."

I stiffened myself, forcing the tremble out of my limbs. "How the hell do you know that?"

"It's what they do," Bastion murmured. "It's what they are. Get it out of your head, Graves. Never. Mention. The Eldest. Again."

A sound of movement at the mouth of the alley caused me to jerk – but it was only Prudence, her boots scuffing the ground as she walked towards us.

"Not another word," Bastion hissed.

I nodded at him, then at Prudence, and as she

approached I sighed in relief. All she had in her hand was a paper bag. There was no way she could fit a puppy and a lamb in there. But without those offerings, would the casting still work?

"We'll have to make do," Prudence said, as if sensing my question. She pushed the paper bag into my hands and dug into her pockets for a little box of chalk. "And you cast the circle this time. About time you learned to do it yourself."

She was right. If I wanted to prove my worth to the Lorica, I needed to be able to do things on my own. I couldn't help feel a thrill, that this would be some of the first real magic I'd ever perform, shadowstepping aside. But I didn't know where to start. Eh. Monkey see, monkey do.

"Funny, isn't it?" I said. "And convenient, how all these gods have their tethers in Valero. I mean, what makes us so important? Why do they come here?"

"Actually," Prudence said, "the gods have multiple tethers, everywhere, mainly places with larger magical populations. That's probably why they're so grumpy all the time. Imagine living in a house that had six front doors, and people were always knocking on all of them."

Ah. Well that made more sense. I could only hope that Hecate wouldn't be that unhappy to see us.

I got on the ground and traced the best circle I could make, the way I'd seen Thea do it. I glanced up every so often, checking on both Bastion and Prudence's faces, but they were impassive. Whatever I was doing seemed to be up to standards.

"Do I – I saw Thea drawing sigils." I scratched the back of my head. "Should I put, like, stars and stuff?"

Bastion snorted. I ignored him. Typical of him to try and pull his schoolyard bully schtick here, but this was too interesting for me, something I didn't want him spoiling with his casual dickery.

"It isn't necessary," Prudence said, getting down on her haunches. "A lot of it has to do with belief and effort. Some fundamental knowledge of arcane imagery helps, sure, but what really fuels magic is whether you think you'll be able to make it happen." She grinned – it was more of a smirk, really – and scratched the side of her nose. "If you think a couple of moons and stars will help strengthen your circle, then you should go ahead and add them."

And I did just that. Whereas Thea's circle had looked like a precise mathematical formula, the magical chalk equivalent of the Vitruvian man, mine looked like something a kid would draw in the playground after they got bored of hopscotch.

Still, it made me proud. I capped it off with what I thought looked like a cool little flame, and a smiley face. I risked another glance at Bastion's face. He had one eyebrow raised, and what I thought looked like a mingling of both ridicule and approval in his expression. Eh. Good enough.

"That works," Prudence said. "Okay, bring out the reagents."

I sifted through the paper bag, glad that we didn't have to sacrifice anything living to access Hecate's domicile, when my fingers came across something clammy and cold. I lifted it out of the bag and grimaced.

"A lamb chop?"

Bastion scoffed. "Really, Prudence? You think that's going to work?"

"You got a better idea?" Prudence snapped. "You try and find me a black ewe this time of night. Besides, Thea keeps talking about how the kid has potential. What matters is how well he can pull this off."

Maybe that put a little bit of a lift in my chin, but it was good to know that somebody at least had some faith in me. "I mean, the entity Thea and I visited just wanted a bunch of fortune cookies."

"Yeah," Prudence said. "Hecate's more of a traditionalist. You can imagine why we don't make more of an effort to seek her out, but she knows things we can't really learn anywhere else. Of course, communing with her comes with its own obstacles, but we'll get to that."

I nodded and kept digging through the bag. The only things left in there were a bottle of honey shaped like a bear, along with a little baggie of dog biscuits. I held them both up.

"Cute."

Bastion shook his head. "Seriously."

"I swear, Brandt," Prudence said. "Not another word."

The lamb chop went next to the dead pigeon, two cold bits of meat literally chilling on the pavement. I tipped out a couple of dog biscuits onto the ground, crushing them underfoot for good measure, then uncapped the bottle and drizzled honey over the entire mess. I looked to the far end of the alley, grateful that it was so dark, because how the hell were we supposed to explain all this to anyone who walked by?

I stared at my hands dumbly, then realized that this was the last part of the trick. This I wasn't so keen about.

"Needs to be done," Prudence said, somehow always mindful of the processes going on in my own brain. "Brandt," she said, holding up a hand.

Wordlessly, Bastion pulled a switchblade from out of his jacket pocket. I didn't question why one of the Lorica's most powerful Hands needed to have a knife on his person, but maybe it made him feel safe. Or, knowing Bastion and his fondness for that leather jacket, cooler, a bit more dangerous.

"Just a nick," Prudence said. "Just prick the end of your finger. That should do it."

I took out the blade, testing the sharpness of it against my palm when I remembered. "I saw Thea mumbling things, too. That I don't know how to do."

"Again, doesn't matter," Bastion said. I had to admit, I was surprised he was even contributing. "Make up the words as you go. Recite a poem, or the lyrics from a song. Doesn't matter. The point is that your voice declares your intent and conviction. What the words are, that's immaterial. The entity needs to know that you want to see her badly enough."

"Right," I said, nodding at his instructions. "Here we go."

The knife's point didn't hurt as much as I thought it would, a bead of blood welling up where I pressed it against my skin. It hissed as it hit the center of the circle, and a thrum of energy rushed through me. It was working.

Shadowstepping was one thing, but this was another entirely. I was opening a door to another world. I mean, okay, functionally I did that when I shadowstepped too, but hush. This was actual ritual magic. I tucked the knife into my jeans pocket, still transfixed on the smoldering spot on the asphalt that was once a drop of my blood.

"Puppy Yum biscuits are the perfect anytime treat for your furry friends," I droned, reading off the back of the packet. "Made with only the best organic beef and lamb, Puppy Yum biscuits also contain mutt-friendly grains and fiber, for – "

Something – I couldn't tell you what, exactly – shifted in the air around me. Which was strange, because the only physical change I noticed came from the ground. A crack in the center of the circle grew larger and longer, at a speed alarming enough that I stepped back. The pigeon, the raw lamb chop, the biscuits, all of it slipped into the earth as the slit grew bigger, then formed into a shape that was all too familiar, and eerie. A mouth.

Black lips, black teeth, and deeper in the hole, a snaking black tongue. The faint sound of humming faded as the bizarre, oversized ebony human mouth yawned silently, then opened wider. Then it began to scream.

Dozens of voices, all discordant, issued from that same chasm. I whipped around to check, but no one outside the alley seemed attracted to the horrific noise, and from the leaves and debris tumbling in the streets, I saw why. Without warning a storm had whipped up again, ripping through the city once more, the roar of wind and thunder mingling with the black mouth's screams.

Lei Kung might not have been one of the big guns, as Prudence put it, but the world prepared to grieve for every entity it lost. It brought the pressure of properly doing this communion bearing down on us even harder: we needed to set things right.

The storm sent one last gentle reminder. Cracking like the end of days, a flash of lightning seared the streets as it struck a utility pole. An explosion to match the thunder rumbled through the block, and the resultant shower of sparks was the last light in the vicinity as the power went out. Yeah. We had to set things right, and fast.

The mouth kept on singing its terrible dirge, voiced by a choir culled from hell itself. One voice sounded like a man being skinned alive, another, a child crying, and another, a woman mourning. They wailed all at once. I grimaced as I turned to Bastion and Prudence, both of them gritting their teeth against the noise. Only we could hear it, then, the shrieking portal, this mouth from hell.

"That's the doorway?" I shouted over the din.

"Get in," Prudence yelled back.

"Ladies first." I'd never seen Bastion afraid. He was still making every effort to look unruffled, of course, but I could tell by the lines in the creases of his eyes that he was at least deeply unsettled.

"Fuck's sake," I said. I don't know what came over me then, but I like to think that it's part of what makes me such an unpredictable and wildly attractive individual. I soldiered forward and stepped into the portal myself.

I already told you how it feels to shadowstep, how it can be cold, and to a point, somewhat suffocating. And I told you how entering Arachne's portal was slow, laborious, like swimming through molasses or, quite literally, walking through spiderwebs. This? This was so much worse.

Traveling through Hecate's portal was like jumping down the spit-slick throat of some colossal beast, sliding further and further down this steep, pulsing tunnel. It felt as if I was smothered in saliva, even though my skin and clothes remained dry. A hot wind blew up and down the tunnel, like something breathing. The worst was the darkness, the total blackness of it all, of not knowing where this infernal gullet began and ended.

Then it came to a stop.

I blinked, and the gloom was lifted. Bastion and Prudence were standing to either side of me, as dazed as I was, but none the worse for wear. We were in a meadow, the tall grass of it rustling in a gentle breeze, under a massive field of stars in a night sky as black as ink. It was so idyllic that it felt all the more unnatural. Wrong.

It didn't make sense, for example, for us to be surrounded by so many chains dangling from out of the sky, suspended, it seemed, from the stars themselves. They drifted lazily in the breeze, as innocuous as vines, yet clinking ominously as they moved.

Around us, where the sound of the wind should have been, came an unnameable, wordless chattering of so many voices, just loud enough to make out, yet never loud enough to understand. And from far afield, or sometimes, from the sky itself, came the playing of pipes, here discordant, there melodious, alien and distant. And then she stepped out of the darkness.

Statuesque. That was the first word I would have used to describe Hecate, and not just for her height, either, but her sheer majestic presence. Her skin had all the color of a marble statue, pale in the starlight. She wore a cloak as black as the night itself, now shifting in the breeze, but at times moving as if of its own accord. What looked like beads and gemstones sparkled from the folds of her garment, but I blinked again and knew that they were stars.

Small lengths of chain clinked and dangled from her cloak, the end of it hemmed in what looked like emerald green thread, but I recognized it as the grass we were standing on. Her robe was a miniature of our exact surroundings, a microcosm. I squinted and saw the figures stitched onto it, little effigies of myself, and Bastion, and Prudence, and among them, a copy of Hecate herself, wearing her own cloak made of stars and sky.

"Stop looking," Prudence whispered. "Not the cloak."

I blinked and looked away, with some grim knowing that if my gaze lingered I'd be staring closer and harder, forever, that it would drive me mad.

Hecate fixed us with glassy eyes, both of them in complete blackness, the whites of them missing. She was beautiful, but there was nothing specific about her that I could remark on, nothing to remember her beauty by. It felt as though her features shifted with every passing second, my mind struggling to keep up with every form her face assumed. Again I wondered how long it would take before one of us went completely insane just from standing there.

"Three of them approach," she said, one mouth speaking in many voices. "Three, like us."

They weren't there before, and then they were, two exact duplicates of the entity, flanking the original. I rubbed at my temple with one hand, as if that could stave off madness.

"They come seeking answers," said one Hecate.

"Yet they do not know the questions," said another.

"Dude." Bastion elbowed me in the ribs. "Say something."

I cleared my throat, stepped forward, and puffed out my chest. "Hecate. We've come to bring justice to your kind. Your brothers have been murdered. Help us, and we will ensure that this will never happen again."

"Help you. Yes." The three entities raised hands to their chins, cupping their elbows in the palms of their free hands. "And if we help, we suppose your precious Lorica will be our armor, your assurance that we will be unharmed in future." Their shadows lengthened against the grass, though they didn't grow any taller. "But what help," she said, her voices trembling, "does a god need? What can a fleshling like you possibly offer for our protection?"

I stammered wordlessly, hating that I was intimidated by her display of power. It was just the *Wizard of Oz*, as far as I could tell, her posturing, with her booming voice and her shadows. But I had to remind myself: that was all from a movie, a book. This creature before me wasn't a man behind a curtain. It was a deity, a goddess of magic, and without having to be told, I knew she was the most dangerous thing I had ever encountered in my life.

"Hecate, please," Prudence said, her voice imploring. "We need to stop the murders. We've given you your offerings."

"Pale substitutions." Hecate examined her fingers, her facsimiles doing the same. "You are fortunate we allowed you into our domicile all the same."

Prudence cowed at that, as if even she had to admit that the entity was right. Which she was. We brought Arachne the cookies she wanted, but the base sacrifices we offered Hecate were barely even up to snuff. Something cold trailed along my spine. We didn't have exactly what Hecate wanted. Did that mean she could demand whatever she wanted of us?

"At the very least," Hecate said, "you might compensate with entertainment. We haven't had visitors in so very long." Out of all her features, I could finally make out her lips. Beautiful, full, and painted black. They quirked in a smile.

"Perhaps you could favor us with a game."

The grass rustled as both Bastion and Prudence shifted their posture around me. Clearly I wasn't the only one who was uncomfortable with the idea.

"We didn't come here to bargain with our lives," Prudence said, her fist clenched. In the starlight, I could see the faint traces of blue energy pulsing across her knuckles.

"Then why have you come to our domicile empty-handed?"

This wasn't going well. I whirled around, expecting to find the portal there the way Arachne's gossamer door had been waiting behind us, but I hadn't seen any gateways since we'd entered Hecate's realm. We were at the entity's mercy.

"Then if there are no more objections, we shall play our game. There is only one rule." All three Hecates lifted their hands to the sky. The ground began to rumble. As one, they spoke.

"Try not to die." Hecate's smiles grew wider. "It spoils the fun."

Chapter 13

The rumbling grew louder with each passing second, the tremors so powerful they nearly threw me off my feet. A crack of thunder emanated from within the very ground itself. Spires of rock exploded from the earth, showering us in a rain of dirt and debris.

The perfect emerald sheen of the meadow tore into ruin as the spires rose higher and higher, tall enough to block each of Hecate's apparitions from view, then taller still until the tips of them disappeared into the sky.

I looked at Prudence, then at Bastion uncertainly, both of them already drawing closer, backs to each other. Prudence's hands were close to her chest, her fingers crooked like talons prepared to strike, each of them bathed in pulsing blue fire.

Nearby, Bastion crouched closer to the ground, as if readying himself for another surprise. His power had very subtle physical manifestations, as far as I knew, small flashes of light, which only led the unfamiliar to underestimate him. To all the Lorica, Bastion was a walking engine of destruction, and all our issues aside, I knew he would put up a good fight.

And me, I huddled to join the other two, regretting that I hadn't begged Thea harder to teach me a spell, something explosive I could use to defend myself. I watched the chains and the shadows that the stars cast across them, readying myself to run.

The spires around us, I realized, weren't spires at all, but columns of rock engraved with uniform grooves running all along their lengths. They surrounded us like sentinels, keeping us confined in a space no bigger than a baseball field. Encircled and entrapped, I noticed that the arrangement of this all looked dreadfully familiar.

A colosseum. Hecate had erected a colosseum from the earth itself.

Prudence spun around, her head lifted to the sky, face twisted in anger. "Surely you don't expect us to fight each other," she cried out. "That will never happen, Hecate."

The air wavered at the far end of the entity's makeshift stadium, and each of her three simulacra appeared at once.

All three spoke. "Each other? How droll. You will play with us."

The apparitions lifted their hands. The chains hanging from the stars reared back and coiled like enormous snakes, clanking with the horrible metal scrape of machinery.

As one, the apparitions spoke. "Let the games begin."

They raised their hands, opening their palms in a slow, deliberate gesture, and the chains came shrieking out of the night. One of them struck the ground just by us, the ground exploding in tufts of grass and clumps of dirt as the huge metal links ate their way into the earth. The chain shook itself off, as if collecting itself from a momentary daze, then lifted back again, rearing to strike, like a viper.

"Scatter," Prudence yelled.

We didn't need to be told twice. We broke into three directions, but even as we ran my heart sank when I saw that there were so many of them, these sentient chains dangling from the sky. What I hadn't counted on was how methodically my colleagues were working to even the odds.

One of the chains, massive and cumbersome, just barely missed Prudence, and its weight and size drove its bulk into the earth. Without uttering a word, Prudence turned and drove her fist into the nearest link. The metal fell apart in a brilliant burst of blue energy, the link snapping from the tremendous force of her power. The chain went limp.

So there it was: these things were alive, somehow, and breaking off a large enough part of the chains was enough to deactivate them. Each functioned as its own being, and dealing enough damage would be enough to "kill" it. Not that I could help at all in that department.

Bastion demonstrated that on his own, and he didn't even have to be sly about waiting for the things to embed themselves in the ground before striking. He gauged until they were close enough, then cleaved his open hand in an arc. It looked for all the world like he was making a vain attempt at karate chopping thin air, but the effect was immediate. It was as if a massive, invisible sword had cleaved its way through two of the chains, severing them in half and sending the ruined tangle of links crashing to the ground. Each of those links was the size of a car. The stadium rumbled.

"Stop standing there with your dick hanging out," Bastion shouted. "Just shadowstep and stay out of danger." For once I agreed with him completely, and maybe I even heard a trace of concern in his voice.

I stayed out of the way, watching and clinging to the wall behind me as more of the chains crashed to the ground, as my protectors capably disabled and destroyed every threat that approached us. The three Hecates motioned continuously with their hands, sending salvo after shrieking salvo of the chain-beasts after us. I was expecting her to be enraged by how many of her pets had fallen, but she hardly seemed bothered at all. Hecate – all three of her – they were laughing, with all the glee of a child at play.

Then all three turned their heads, fixed me with six wet, black eyes, and smiled.

"Fuck."

Six hands extended towards me, fingers like talons outstretched, and as one the chains suspended in the sky soared into life, screaming through the air in a groaning frenzy of metal and carnage. From somewhere in the stadium I could hear Prudence and Bastion shouting, warning me to run. I pressed up against the wall, the stone of the columns cold against my back, the sweat like ice on my forehead. I waited.

As the chains drew nearer they coiled into a twisting slurry of living metal, like a giant, writhing spire that came to a point, a gleaming, gray tentacle. Hecate's laughter danced across the stadium as the chains rushed for me, aiming, I thought, for my heart. Their shadow approached, a spreading pool of darkness beneath this comet of steel. There was only place I knew to go. I stepped.

I rushed through the Dark Room, knowing that my timing had to be precise to make sure this would have even a chance of working. I emerged from the shadows cast against the far wall by Hecate's apparitions. The three of them looked around the colosseum in synchronized bewilderment, searching for a trace of me. By all appearances, I had simply blinked out of existence. They hadn't spotted me standing behind them just yet.

But the chains had.

I only had time to look for my destination before the chains hit their mark. As I shadowstepped again I heard Hecate scream in three voices, the noise cut abruptly by the collision of so much metal against earth, then against stone. I emerged at the far end of the stadium, panting from the effort of both running and taking the shadowsteps, and watched mouth agape as the hulking mass of twisted metal kept scraping across the ground, grinding its way through the side of the colosseum like an airplane skidding across a runway.

The wall didn't stop its descent, and the stone columns of the colosseum cracked, crumbled, and broke apart under the gargantuan assault. A fresh breeze blew in through the breach made by the tangled mass of chains, all of them rendered still and lifeless now that their master was nowhere to be found. The only trace that Hecate had ever been here was the long smear of blood spattered ungracefully across the ground and the rubble.

Bastion threw his hands up to his temples,

clutching at his hair, his eyes huge. "Holy shit, Graves. What did you – holy shit." I could almost hear what he was really trying to say: "That was awesome." Or maybe it was just wishful thinking on my part.

But then Prudence spoke up. "Good going, Dustin, but – she was our contact." Her hands were at her waist, her face grim as she assessed the situation. "Even if she survived that, I don't think Hecate's going to be very happy."

"Don't be so sure."

The voice echoed from around the stadium. The earth began trembling again, a slow tremor, at first, as the stone columns began to crumble, not into dust and rubble, but into shards and fragments of bone. Had this colosseum been built out of the skeletons of those who didn't win at Hecate's game? I wrapped one hand around my wrist, feeling for my bones through my skin, and swallowed thickly.

As the columns receded, the broken bones fell into squat piles, until we could finally see the sky around us again. The cool breeze of Hecate's endless night blew across a meadow left grassless and scarred by her chain-beasts. Then out of nowhere a pale green fire consumed the bones, the flames emanating a faint chill.

Within moments the bones were burned to nothing, dissolving into the earth, and fresh, dewy grass sprang from the ground, green and vibrant as spring, like death completing its cycle.

It made no sense at all, but in the maddening perpetual midnight of Hecate's domicile, I was starting to worry at how my mind accepted it as being totally logical.

One pile of bones remained. I thought nothing of it until Prudence and Bastion crowded around me again, flanking me, hands raised at the ready.

The bones rattled, then started snaking across the ground.

"Great," Bastion grumbled. "What is it this time?"

The bones caused the grass to sway as they passed through, rustling against it the way an animal might in tall rushes. Prudence held a hand out against my chest, a protective stance, as the bones began to pile on top of each other, haphazardly, it seemed, until I realized that they were reassembling themselves into the size and shape of a skeleton.

"Hecate," Prudence said. "If you're around here somewhere, if this is another one of your games, I swear I'll punch that thing to bonemeal before you can – "

The skull came last, topping the macabre assortment of self-levitating bones, and its jawbones clacked as it opened its hinges to speak.

"No more games," the skeleton said in Hecate's voice. "You've already won."

I wiped the sweat off my brow, the moisture gone cool in the meadow's air. "So," I ventured. "No hard feelings about me crushing your body?

Er, bodies?"

The skeleton's laughter was good-natured, and deeply eerie considering the context and the messenger. "None at all, fleshling. You cannot kill us here. Not by normal means, anyway. You have earned our curiosity. And perhaps – a gift."

I had no real way of telling, but I knew that Hecate's skull was smiling at me. It was creepy as hell. More unsettling, though, was how tiny particles began moving across her bones, like thousands of ants marching over her skeleton.

"Oh God," Bastion muttered to himself. My thoughts were very much the same.

They weren't insects, but bits of Hecate's flesh, reassembling and knitting over her skeleton, filling out her frame and reforming her body. My stomach churned as muscle, sinew, and fat stitched itself into existence, as her organs materialized seemingly out of thin air, then began pulsing, beating. All the while the death's head of her skull kept grinning at us, until it too began closing over with ribbons and ridges of new flesh. Grossest thing I'd ever seen, at that point.

"Don't be so perturbed," Hecate said. "We only take this form because it is so familiar to you. This is what you fleshlings look like on the inside, is it not?"

"Sure," Prudence said cautiously. "But we don't tend to see our own insides unless it involves injury. Or death."

Hecate scoffed, something that looked more

natural now that her lips were growing back. As was her skin, I noted. Small mercies.

"You fleshlings really are so touchy about death."

"With all due respect," I said, "we kind of have to be, Hecate. We can't do – well, whatever it is you're doing now. We get one life, and that's it."

Hecate nodded, her new head of hair tumbling with its perfect raven locks as she did. "A fine point. But you were never in any real danger. We wouldn't have killed you. We can't go around killing every mage who steps into our domicile. Then we would have wizards knocking on our door demanding justice every hour."

Sensing that we were probably mostly out of danger, Bastion finally relaxed his stance. "You could have fooled us. Didn't seem like you were holding back."

Hecate laughed again, her body now fully formed, breasts and hair and beautiful skin unmarred, like it all hadn't just been pulverized by something the size and velocity of a runaway train just minutes before. Her cloak of midnight stitched itself back together over the milky pallor of her body. It draped around her shoulders, and I realized that I couldn't tell where her hair ended and the cloak began. From where I stood, both, it seemed, were speckled with little stars.

"You fleshlings are more capable than you think. We were confident." She raised a finger, crooking it in my direction. "But this little one has surprised us. We have never seen anything quite like him."

She snapped her fingers. A ball of sickly green flame burned in the air right before her. I stepped back on reflex. Didn't she say no more games? But the flames receded as suddenly as they'd appeared, leaving in their place a massive book suspended in midair. Its cover was the blackest black I'd ever seen, like something from out of the void. Hecate spread her arms and the book began flipping through its pages.

"That's her own grimoire," Bastion said, whispering into my ear, pressing against me in what felt like such an unnecessarily conspiratorial way.

"Really," I deadpanned. "What tipped you off?"

"Imagine what she keeps there," Prudence said. "A goddess of magic. Imagine what she knows."

"Quite a lot, actually," Hecate said distractedly, more to the air than to our huddle. "Enough that we can hear everything that's spoken inside our realm." She lifted her head to peek above the grimoire's massive pages, giving us an odd smile. "We need to keep things secure, after all."

The air around her wavered, and again there were three Hecates, all staring intently at the grimoire. It rustled through its pages so quickly that nothing human could have caught even a glimpse of its contents. Then the three of them each stabbed a finger at the book, and the pages stopped flipping.

"Here it is."

I stood on tiptoes, trying to figure out what "it" was, exactly.

"Curious," one Hecate said. "The little one steps between shadows," said another. "Yet it isn't all that he can do," said the last.

I shrugged and threw up my hands. "That's honestly all I know how to do. I'm good at stepping because I'm good at hiding and – I guess at running away from things."

It was strange how poignant the words pouring out of my own mouth were sounding to my ears, but I filed it all away for later inspection. I really was good at running away, from a lot of things. Even the good things.

"Thea – my mentor once told me that the magic we know, that we're good at, it comes from who we are as people. That's who I am."

Hecate's mouth twisted in distaste, black lips bent into a sneer. "You fleshlings are so limited by what you think, what you believe, so much that you forget how resilient you are, how you can adapt, and change, and evolve, and survive. Like cockroaches, you are. You run and you run, little one." All three Hecates tilted their heads. "When will you stop running and turn to face your darkness? When will you take control?"

Prudence and Bastion shifted at my side, their

expressions flat, but curious. I didn't know if Hecate was speaking to how I was dealing with the whole business about the murders, or my own death, or hell, my relationship with my father, but what she said was making sense in a couple of painful ways.

When I started working for the Lorica, I never guessed my life would get sorted out by an encounter with a manifestation of an ancient Greek deity. This was better than a shrink, but at least ten times as dangerous. And probably a few dozen times more terrifying.

"The shadows are your friends, Dustin Graves." Hecate waved her hand. The book and the apparitions all disappeared in a cloud of green smoke. She stepped forward, into her own shadow – then appeared inches from my face.

I stumbled back. What the hell? She just – she just shadowstepped.

"Embrace them," Hecate said, her voice like velvet, her eyes solid pools of liquid black. "Immerse in them. Understand the darkness, and it will be yours to command."

"I – I don't understand."

Hecate shook her head. "You will in time. For now, remember. You are in charge of your own destiny. There is no future but the one you create." She reached out and stroked a lock of hair away from my forehead. Her hand was soft, warm. Her touch was gentle.

"Dust," Bastion muttered, his voice ringing

with warning.

Maybe it's crazy to say it now, but more than anything the entire night – more than the living chains and the dissonant song of pan flutes, and how the mad goddess had stitched herself to life right in front of us – this was what I found strangest of all. The way she tousled my hair like a mother would, the way she smiled at me. The way the pools of shadow that were her eyes twinkled as she smiled – the way they suddenly filled with stars.

Prudence lunged for me. "Dustin, no."

"Embrace the shadows," Hecate whispered. "The Dark Room is your home. Take comfort in it. No more running."

"I don't understand," I breathed.

"You need to get it through your thick skull, fleshling." Hecate smiled. "The door opens from both ends."

She touched my forehead with the tip of a single finger. The warmth of her skin escalated until it burned like a coal, then like molten steel, a spear-tip fresh from the fire. I screamed, the pain of it stabbing between my eyes, piercing my skull, setting my brain aflame.

The stars in Hecate's eyes swirled as she muttered, the pair of them like twin galaxies. The pain ripped through my skin, every cell in my body ablaze with agony. I screamed, and screamed, and screamed.

Then all at once, the stars went out.

Chapter 14

When I came to, it was dark, and I was on my back on something soft. Comfortable, almost, and padded. For the glimmer of a second I convinced myself that I was in a coffin, my body pressed against the padded interior. I gasped and cried out.

Ah. Of course. It was a bed, and not a coffin at all. It took a while for me to register that I should open my eyes. The lids of them were heavier, like I'd been drugged. I forced my eyes open slowly and breathed easier when I saw that I was just in my bedroom. Not at my apartment, mind you, but the new place designated for me at Lorica HQ. Room 17B. I let my head flop back onto my pillow and sighed. I was content to be resting, and alone.

"Dude. It's okay."

Except that I wasn't. I started again, not even realizing that someone else was in the room with me, and for some reason my instinct was to draw the covers up around me. Not that I was naked, as far as I could tell, but there was something extra vulnerable about being caught in bed, on my back, my soft underbelly exposed. I'd already been killed once. Laying on my back on flat surfaces could still be unsettling for me.

"I said it's okay," Bastion said.

A hand looped reassuring fingers around my wrist, and to my own surprise, I didn't recoil from his touch. I opened my eyes again, thinking I was hallucinating, but I wasn't. There he was, in a chair by my bed, standing – rather, sitting guard like a sentinel. Sebastion Brandt, once an enemy, and now – my caretaker? Nurse? I blinked the thought away.

"I'm okay," I said, or rather, tried to say. The words tumbled out of my mouth in an unintelligible mumble, my tongue leaden, my throat parched. I tried to say something else, but all I could do was produce hoarse puffs of breath. I gasped, mentally reminding myself not to panic.

"It's okay," Bastion repeated, and I knew he was only trying to be helpful, but there were only so many times he could say that before I stopped believing him. Then he reached for something at my side, fumbling, and I heard the gorgeous sound of water splashing into a glass. I could taste it before I even saw it. Bastion brought the glass to my lips. Water never tasted so good.

"Careful. Slow."

"Mmhmm," I managed between gulps of water. "Thank you." Ah. I could finally say things. Much better.

"You've been out for a while."

I licked my lips, glancing at the glass in his hand, eager for more water. "I figured. Thirsty as hell. Would you mind?" Bastion nodded obligingly, pouring me another drink. "How long have I been out?"

"Let's see," he said, gently tipping water into my mouth. "I want to say it's been about – "

His eyes rolled up to the ceiling as he held one hand out, counting off on his fingers, mouthing numbers silently. "I guess about twenty-seven hours now."

I almost choked on my water. "What? How is that possible?"

Bastion shrugged. "Guess you were exhausted. Prue says it was the effort of shadowstepping so much in such a short period of time. My guess is that whatever Hecate did took a lot out of you." He replaced the glass on the side table. "Thea says it was both."

"What did she do to me?"

"Nothing horrible, as far as we can tell. Call me crazy but I think she liked you. But whatever it was knocked you out on the spot. Had to carry you here."

"Had to?" I blinked again, my eyes focusing on Bastion's face. Somehow he didn't look as annoying as he used to, maybe because he wasn't making such an effort to be a douche, for once. "You mean you carried me yourself?"

I could see him redden. "Don't flatter yourself. You needed help, and I wasn't going to make Prue do it herself." He scratched his nose, the back of his neck, the redness still in his cheeks. "Thea told us to take care of you. I don't need her on my ass, too." He scratched his eyebrow next, turning his gaze up to the ceiling again, then sighed, his shoulders slumping just so slightly. "And fine, maybe I thought you deserved a break. What you did with Hecate back there? That was risky. And dangerous. But it paid off."

I did my best not to smile, but Bastion was paying me a compliment. I never thought I'd see the day.

"I – I guess it was kind of badass." He cleared his throat. "Good job, rookie." Then he furrowed his brow and leaned closer to the bed. "But you tell anyone I was ever nice to you and I swear I'll snap you in half. Won't take me much work, either."

I smiled again. "Fine. Our little secret."

The hardness receded from Bastion's face, and he even allowed himself to smile a little, giving me a small nod. But that all washed away when a knock came at the door.

It creaked open slowly – just like the door at

my apartment, like the Lorica somehow knew to pluck even that detail from out of my mind – and Thea poked her head in. The room seemed brighter somehow, and I knew at that point to chalk it up to her presence. Something about the woman just oozed radiance. The sight of her, especially her sudden, eager smile, was certainly enough to cheer me up, even a little.

"Knock knock," she said, stepping in, the bright white of her clothes bringing even more illumination into the bedroom.

I smiled back. "Thought it was Prudence."

"Not quite," Thea said. "She's out for work."

Bastion nodded at her in greeting. "Sup," he said, in that half-bored drone he liked to use. "He just got up."

Thea nodded. "I can take over from here. You should go grab some lunch. It's late."

Bastion shifted in his chair. "It's cool, I can stay."

"It's fine, Brandt. I'd like some one-on-one time with Dustin here. And you've been here for hours. Prudence tells me you got in at nine and just disappeared."

Bastion stared at the ground, his ears reddening again. I quirked an eyebrow but said nothing. We were getting along well enough that I didn't want to rub salt in his wounds.

It was flattering, though, that he'd spent all that time watching over me. Either Bastion took Thea's orders much more seriously than I'd thought, or, and this was the truly horrifying part – maybe he was a good guy on the inside after all.

The chair's legs scraped against the floor as Bastion got up abruptly. His eyes flitted from the side table, to Thea's face, then mine. "I'll – see you around, I guess."

"Thanks, Bastion," I said. "For everything."

He smiled, a small one that I was almost sure he didn't want Thea seeing, then stalked straight out the door. Thea shook her head and shrugged.

"He's a good boy, but really preoccupied with putting up a tough front. I'm glad to see that he's finally getting used to you. Or the other way around."

"Yeah, I get what you mean. Never thought I'd say this, but he's actually okay."

"And it looks like you're getting used to more than just your colleagues here at the Lorica, Dustin." Thea smoothed the back of her skirt under her thighs as she took Bastion's chair. "I heard you cast your first circle."

I lit up. "I did. Prudence told you?"

Thea nodded, her eyes bright, smile as proud as a soccer mom. "The smiley face was a nice touch. I heard the entity gave you something else as well."

That was right. I wasn't sure why I didn't bother checking earlier. I reached for my forehead, certain that a hole had been bored straight to the center of my brain, but there was nothing there. The skin was smooth, unburned, unbroken. I craned my neck, trying to get a glimpse of my face in my drinking glass, when Thea spoke up.

"You're fine. Nothing there. I know it feels like something's wrong, but truthfully it looks like you did something right. That's the second entity you've met who's granted you a favor."

My eyes went wide. "Really? That thing where Hecate fried my brain from the outside. That was a favor?"

Thea held up her hands and shrugged. "Gods work in mysterious ways." She chuckled, clearly pleased with herself.

"Very funny." I rubbed at my forehead again. "Whatever she did, it hurt like hell. But I'm not sure what I got out of it."

"You never can be. All you know is that an entity has favored you. Maybe she's granted you some hidden knowledge. Or you might be able to call on her in a time of need." She rubbed at her chin. "The question is whether she'll answer. She's a fickle one, that Hecate."

"So I've been told. Kind of crazy, too."

"Right. Which is why she didn't even give us any information on the murders."

"Maybe she did? She said to – " I mouthed the words before I spoke them, then realized how irrelevant they were to anything we were working on. "To embrace the shadows. To understand the darkness."

"Yeah. Still nothing. Maybe it'll make sense

later. But listen, Dust." She clasped her hands together, leaning forward. "You've been with us such a short time, but you've already done so much. I really am proud of you."

That caught me off guard. I gawped for a second before she spoke again.

"Sometimes I wonder, you know, how my life would be if things had gone differently with my kids. I wonder if they would have grown up magical. I wonder if they would have done as well as you."

Something twinged in my chest. Thea never spoke about her children. I told her what I felt. "Knowing who their mom is, I'm sure they would have done even better."

Thea smiled, and something seemed to twinkle in her eye. But then she rose from her seat, her eyebrows furrowing as her gaze went to my shoulder. Before I could say anything, she struck me, swatting at my arm with her open hand.

"Ow." I looked up at her, bewildered. "Wow. You're really bad at taking compliments."

"Hmm?" she said absently, looking into her palm. "Oh, no. It's nothing. Just a spider. Lorica's an old building, you know how it is." She brushed her hands off, letting the squashed arachnid fall to the ground. Thea smiled. "Someone will pick that up."

"Yeah, okay." I rubbed my shoulder. "Thanks."

"For now I need you to rest up. Get better.

Looks like we'll have to set our sights elsewhere. Maybe we'll send you to commune with another entity."

I groaned.

"Cheer up, Dust. Maybe you'll be granted yet another favor. The entities seem to love you."

I pulled the covers up over my chest, honestly wanting to slip them all the way up over my head. "No more favors. I'm still reeling from the last one."

Thea chuckled. "Some Tylenol should fix that. Get some rest, Dust. And get in touch with one of us if you're hungry. Someone will come. You shouldn't be up and about yet."

I nodded and gave her a weak salute. Thea smiled again, then shut the door quietly behind her. Food was the last thing on my mind. I just wanted more sleep. I riffled through my side table – whether the meds were there because of Bastion or the Lorica's bizarre sentience I couldn't be sure, but whoever it was, thank you thank you – chugged some pills, then crawled back under the sheets. Twenty-seven hours? Hah. My head, hell, my entire body still felt like it'd been run over by a truck.

When I opened my eyes again, I still had no real conception of time. Thea had dismissed Bastion and told him to grab a late lunch, so I guessed that it must have been mid-afternoon when I woke the first time. But how long had I been asleep since then? What time was it now? I looked around the room, wondering where my cellphone was, and started checking on the side table when the door creaked open again.

"Dust?"

I looked over at the door and perked up instantly. "Herald. Buddy. Old pal."

He returned that with a tight smile, stepping into the room clutching what looked like a large paper cup. A familiar, rich aroma wafted through the air above my bed, into my nostrils, and –

"Is that. Is that coffee?"

"Got it in one. I know you like your coffee. I mean I'm not entirely sure I made it the way you like but – "

"Doesn't matter." I snatched the cup eagerly out of his hands as soon as he and the coffee were within grabbing distance. When did I last have any caffeine? God. Maybe I was addicted.

I blew across the lid, took a tentative sip, then hummed contentedly. "This is so sweet."

"Oh." Herald adjusted his glasses. "Maybe I added too much sugar after all."

"No, no. I meant it's really sweet that you brought me this." I sipped again, savoring the richness, that hint of chocolate and milk. I held up the coffee cup. "You didn't have to, and I really appreciate it."

He shrugged. "It's no bother. I would have come sooner but things have been hectic over in the Gallery."

That was when I noticed that Herald's tie was

looser around his neck, his waistcoat more creased than usual, his hair slightly mussed. Strange. The guy was always so put-together. I took another sip.

"You've been working too hard." I don't know how many times I'd said that to him, but between Herald's responsibilities and his own alchemical experiments, it was a wonder how he hadn't already collapsed from overexertion.

Herald grimaced. He liked to give off the impression that he was stern and stony, but I knew better. "No. I haven't. And anyway, I came to check on you. How are you feeling?"

"Bored." I took another swig of coffee and smacked my lips. "Boring? Pick one." I realized it was true. I'd had enough sleep, and I was aching for something – no, anything to do.

"If you weren't in such a condition I'd take you over to the Gallery, show you some of the new stuff that's rolled in. That wouldn't be boring." He waved his hand around the emptiness of my makeshift apartment. "Well, at least not as boring as this."

"We should go," I said, throwing the covers off. "Like now. I'm better, I promise." As if on cue, my stomach grumbled. "Also, I'm starving. Is there anything to eat?"

Herald glanced at his watch and shrugged. "Well it's almost seven, so I think most people have cleared out by – "

"Seven? What the hell are you still doing at

work?"

He rolled his eyes. "Shut up, Graves. We'll order in, fill you up. Then you can come and check out all of the Gallery's new toys."

Chapter 15

"Wow. Slow down there, tiger."

If I had room in my mouth or energy enough to do so I would have blurted out an aggressive "No." I felt like I hadn't eaten in days and that Thai green beef curry went down fast. It was the good stuff, too, made with coconut milk, and spicy enough to get me forcing more rice down my throat.

I was glad that Herald had the foresight to order three extra helpings of rice. And pad thai, and some spring rolls, all of which I'd devoured. He gave me the leftover half of his red curry, too. I didn't know if he really was full, or if he just felt sorry for me, but I demolished that as well.

I found a moment to actually swallow, and a second to wonder when my body was finally going to realize just how much food I'd dumped into it.

"Let me live my damn life, Herald." I washed it all down with what felt like half a takeout cup of Thai iced tea, that beautifully sweet and creamy stuff that they made with lots of condensed milk. I'd finished mine, too, so technically I was sucking down on Herald's share. He didn't seem to mind, but that didn't keep the look of bemusement off his face.

"Just saying, it could be a shock to your system, the way you're shoving all of that right in your face."

"I know," I conceded. I waved at the table. "But there's nothing left, so there's nothing else for you to worry about just now."

Herald furrowed his brow. "You're not still hungry, are you? We can think of something else to eat later." He was fiddling with something at his workspace, the usual little phials of powder scattered across his desktop. "Well, after I'm done."

I swallowed the rest of the iced tea – sweet nectar, I tell you – and tipped a couple of ice cubes into my mouth, letting them dissolve into cool water. "You aren't seriously still staying, are you? I thought you were heading home after we ate."

Herald scratched his chin, his nails making a faint scraping over his stubble. It was a pretty clear visual indication of how little attention he'd been paying to himself in favor of his work.

"I know, I know," he said, still scratching at his chin. "I'm just trying something different, all right? Itches like hell, but can't hurt to test out a new look."

I shrugged. "Suits you," I said, tossing back the last of my ice cubes.

"Thanks. You can stop worrying. Like I said, this is temporary. There's just been so much happening." He swept his hand around the archives, and I picked up on what he meant.

I hadn't really noticed in my feeding frenzy earlier, but there did seem to be several new installments from the last time I'd visited. I say installments because the Gallery really did look like a museum at times, with all those books and artifacts under glass. Bulletproof, of course, and not because the archivists were trying to keep prying fingers out, but to keep the artifacts in where they belonged. Some of them could get pretty frisky.

"Just saying," I said. "I can see you've been busy, but it doesn't hurt to take a break once in a while."

"Fine. Just finishing this one thing, and I'll head home." His nose crinkled as he furrowed his brow, his glasses slipping again. "You sure you don't want to grab something else on the way out?"

I patted my belly. "Nah. I think I'm good." I probably was. My body was starting to acknowledge the fact that I'd filled it to capacity. "Plus I really don't think Thea wants me roaming around after dark. Especially not now. I'll order something if I get hungry."

Herald nodded at his desk. "There are takeout menus in my left drawer. Or, you know, just look stuff up online. And be sure to deactivate the wards."

"Got it." He'd shown me how to do that earlier on, shortly after I first joined the Lorica. I believed him outright when he said it was crucial. The best case scenario for not deactivating front door security was a pile of ash that used to be a delivery man. Worst case involved being incinerated yourself.

"Make yourself busy," Herald said, shooing me away with one hand.

He bent closer to his desk, and then it was like I wasn't there. His mouth went slack as soon as he started peering through that enormous magnifying glass he kept suspended on a weird multijointed arm bolted to his desk. Kind of like a jeweler's loupe, only way bigger. I'd noticed that the other archivists had their own glasses at their stations as well, so it wasn't an apparatus he used exclusively for his powders. The Lorica liked it when the artifacts were properly sorted and categorized, down to the smallest details.

Actually, sometimes it was the smallest details that mattered. Herald once told me that they found a little box with sigils and etchings carved into its surface. It took some very close inspection to discover that there was a series of buttons embedded in the cube, and that activating them in a particular sequence opened a portal to hell itself, or a place very much like it.

The archivist who figured that out was very lucky, or not at all, depending on how you looked at it. On one hand, he got a sizeable bonus for ensuring that no one at the Lorica got sucked into an infernal dimension. On the other, he made the discovery himself, which meant that he got a glimpse of said dimension. He was never himself after the incident, plus his eyebrows never really grew back.

And that was how I knew to be extra vigilant as I wandered around the Gallery. Arcane acquisition was dangerous enough without the risks of accidentally pressing the wrong button on some mechanical artifact, or of accidentally triggering the contingency spells on a grimoire that alerted its owners when it was in danger.

All of its owners. Seriously. One of the Hounds experienced that, and it was pure chaos. Everyone who had ever owned the grimoire, dead or alive, came all at once to retrieve the relic, fighting the Lorica's people and even each other in increasingly desperate bids to reclaim the book. We really deserved to be paid more.

Not all the artifacts were dangerous, though. There was another book, bound in a strange blue leather, that was actually benign. Helpful, even, which was a word that few could associate with the denizens of the Gallery. It allowed you to store your memories and show them to others, even posthumously.

That made it an excellent method of recording knowledge, whether mundane or magical, in the form of text, photos, or even what looked like videos projected directly on the grimoire's pages. It had other abilities that gave you a glimpse at the public lives of your friends and loved ones, but I was told that most mages who used it ended up just scrying on the people they hated. According to Herald, for a time, everyone wanted a turn on the Phase Book.

Speaking of grimoires, the Book of Plagues was still there, with its doubled protective measures: multiple strands of ensorcelled chains, and a case made out of bulletproof glass. I knew it had no eyes but I could swear it was staring me down, like it knew that I was the one responsible for its incarceration.

"Listen," I said, keeping my voice low. "We both know why you're here, and that's to make sure you don't go around killing people. Okay? You've caused enough trouble as it is."

The book ruffled its pages indignantly, like some irate bird of prey, but it said nothing, because it was a book. That was inaccurate, though. Some enchanters were talented enough to give their creations voices, sometimes through a kind of mouthpiece they could use to communicate, or even through telepathy. Which, incidentally, reminded me of Vanitas. I thought that it couldn't hurt to check on him again, just to see if he'd left his dormant state.

I craned my neck over to Herald, to see if he'd noticed me talking to the grimoire. He was buried in his work, as usual. He was one of the Gallery's favorites, from my understanding, because of the sheer speed and efficiency of his work. I knew that he wanted to get that stuff out of the way to have more time for his alchemical research, which, in itself, was such a flexible branch of magic already. The feats Herald had us Hounds performing with his powders were nothing short of impressive.

Who else could make an instant-action sleeping powder, or that stuff that covered tracks, and all that other dust he created? To be funny I once suggested that we should bootleg some of his inventions and sell them to the normals. Herald got all serious and put me through a fifteen-minute lecture about magic and ethics. Never again.

I always thought that it was a large part of why we became buddies. I joke about him, but I always appreciated that he took the time to explain things about the Veil and the underground to me. Being pretty close in age helped, and we did share common interests in gaming and geek culture. Still, one of the biggest reasons we were friends was our mutual dislike of

Bastion.

It was a couple of days after we met. "Can you imagine the cheek of him? That Brandt moron said he was surprised I dabbled in alchemy. Dabbled! 'I thought you just worked in the archives,' he said. Oh, yeah, that's me, all right. But I'm also an accomplished alchemist, an amateur demonologist, a certified librarian, with a master's degree and everything, thanks very much, not that anybody ever fucking asks, and a level twelve barbarian at my weekly tabletop game, but yeah, sure. 'I just work in the archives.'" I knew then that Herald and I were destined to be the fastest of friends.

I wandered off in search of Vanitas, weaving among the new artifacts, and wrinkled my nose. Even here – perhaps, especially here – there were signs that the city's rodents were still disoriented. I couldn't see a single rat, but here and there were droppings, and everywhere I could distinctly hear the maddening scratching of their paws. I shook myself off. Nature would take its course, and reality would right itself in time. As if in answer, a reminder that there was still work to be done, thunder clapped from somewhere above, hard enough to rattle the building. The lights flickered. I grit my teeth and turned my focus back to the Gallery.

God, there really were a lot of new acquisitions. Had I really been away that long? Under another case was what appeared to be a beat-up cell phone. It didn't even have a touch screen, mind you, just a keypad. My best guess was that it had a spell, maybe several stored on it somewhere, or a couple of demons saved in the contacts. Briefly, I wondered if it was possible to email a fireball as an attachment. Hmm.

Possibly the most disturbing find for the night was a child's crayon drawing of a man and woman, probably their parents. The woman had a knife in her hand, and she kept stabbing the man with it, generating little crayon spurts of blood. That's right, I said "kept stabbing." Who knew how, but the drawings were moving, locked in some macabre animation loop, the little stick figure daddy gushing blood as he held his hands up in a futile defense. I knew it was just a kid's drawing, but it still creeped the hell out of me, especially considering how I had been killed in pretty much the same way.

I finally reached Vanitas's case, ready for the disappointment of once again finding him asleep. Yet something was different. The garnets set into his hilt were brighter, or maybe it only seemed that way because of the light. But then I realized they were shining, exactly how they did whenever he spoke.

"Vanitas?"

The voice rang clear in my mind. "Dustin."

"Holy crap." I pushed my hand up against the glass, hardly caring that I was fogging it up and leaving fingerprints from pressing in so close.

"You're back. Where've you been?"

"I – I'm not sure. Far away."

"What, you mean you were hibernating?"

Vanitas paused, like he was thinking. "Possibly. I haven't fought in ages. I must have been spent. It takes time to replenish my energies, even longer when I'm away from my master."

"I'm not your master."

"Friend, then. But you should know something. You're in danger. There is another of my kind, somewhere here in this room."

"What do you mean, another of your kind?"

"I'm sure you know already. There are other blades like me, made from the same metal, with the same coloration. Some are larger, like claymores, axes." Another pause. "Some are smaller. Like daggers."

My blood went cold. The same metal. I never wanted to consider it but I always thought it strange that I would be so drawn to a sword made out of the same cold bronze that killed me. But this was different. Vanitas was my friend. Wasn't he? More importantly: the sacrificial blade that pierced my heart was here, right in the Gallery?

"Whoever brought it here must mean you harm, Dustin."

I was certain Vanitas was right, but some morbid part of me yearned to see the dagger for myself. It could have held answers, clues about those who had slain me. But why would an implement used by the Black Hand be here at HQ? I leaned against the display case, my mind a flurry.

"I have to find it."

"A terrible notion. But it's your funeral, Graves."

Despite his warning Vanitas guided me among the shelves and display cases, muttering instructions as I drew closer. "Left," he said, "down that way," and "nearly there," until I found the blade.

It was just sitting out there in the open, the dagger with its gold and greenish tinge, set with a gem that looked very much like an eye in its pommel. I remembered that gem flashing in the candlelight the night that dagger plunged into my chest. I remembered how the skin of my palms ripped to ribbons when I held up my hands to ward it away, when the delicate spines along its hilt and guard tore into my fingers.

I stumbled over my own feet as I approached. My heart raced, and I knew sweat was breaking out across my forehead, my arms. You'll pardon the reaction but I wasn't exactly prepared to see my own murder weapon staring me in the face. It wasn't even under glass, like the other artifacts.

"Herald?" I just managed to say his name out loud. "Herald. Where's this from?"

"Hmm?" His voice was distracted at first, but maybe he detected the distress in my tone because I heard movement from his end of the room. "What are you talking about?"

I found myself scoping out the archives for its shadows, an instinctual desire to run already bubbling up inside of me. My hand was clenched into a fist, the other splayed open with fingers against my chest. And my scar, it was hurting.

Herald clapped a hand over my shoulder. "What's up? Is everything all right? You're looking kind of pale." He followed my line of sight to the counter, and his body went rigid, his fingers digging into me.

"That." I didn't need to point. Herald knew exactly what I was referring to. "Where is that from?"

"I thought I put that away," he said. That wasn't the answer I was hoping for.

I shrugged his hand off and backed away. "What do you mean? Isn't this part of the archives? Aren't you supposed to file it like the others?"

Herald held his hands up, his eyes darting left and right, the way someone's eyes do when they're searching for an answer – or making one up.

"They said not to let you see it." He adjusted his glasses again, his hand faintly trembling as he did. "You weren't supposed to see it. I put it away." His voice was trailing off.

"They?" I was aware that my voice was rising to an unreasonable pitch and volume, and I willed myself to calm down. Whoever "they" were, I didn't want them knowing that I'd discovered the very thing they wanted to keep hidden from me.

"Dustin, I can explain. That's why we needed to keep it away from you, because they thought you'd react like this."

"You knew," I said, grunting when I bumped harshly into another display case, my fingers clutching at the counters like I was trying to claw my way out of there. "You knew this thing was right here and you never told me. You knew what happened."

"I can explain," Herald said sternly. "Please. We're trying to find who did this to you."

"No. You're trying to hide. You know, and you're not telling."

"Dust. Please. It's me. You know I wouldn't do that." Herald had come close enough, one hand reaching for my wrist, like he was trying to console me. Or maybe restrain me. I dodged his fingers and stepped into the shadow of a bookshelf.

As the darkness swallowed me up I could hear Herald shouting behind me, and Vanitas pulsing in my head. I couldn't make out their words, not that it mattered anymore. What was going on? It never occurred to me that the Lorica would hide the investigation of my murder from me. Didn't Thea say that they wanted to help bring my killer to justice? What did they know, and why was

Herald involved?

I emerged in one of the pathways radiating out from the Gallery, Herald still speaking to thin air, whirling to find where I had gone. I knew I had scant minutes, maybe seconds to make my move, so I shadowstepped again, far enough as I could see to make my way back to my room.

The Lorica was mercifully empty by then, but moving within the shadows let me bypass most of the corridors anyway. I only hoped there was no one waiting for me in my bedroom. I threw the door open and ran straight for my duffle bag, picking up what essentials I could find. I patted down my jeans, relieved that I had apparently forgotten to give Bastion back his knife, or, alternately, that he'd forgotten to take it from me. I didn't know how to use the thing, but at least I had an option.

I turned for the door. Herald would know to find me here, but I had a head start on him, and if I hurried I could deactivate the failsafes at the entrance and head the hell out of HQ. And go where? I ran a hand through my hair, gritting my teeth in frustration. Somewhere I could clear my head. Someplace I could think. I began to head for the door, but something on the floor drew my attention. Something glimmering.

I stepped closer, then bent down for a better look, and frowned. It was that spider that Thea had killed, the one she swatted off my shoulder earlier. And I wouldn't have noticed it at all if it hadn't been for the gem embedded in its back, a bright green stone the size of a penny.

Arachne. It was one of her children, the ones she trusted with secrets, with harvesting and conveying information. It was perched on my shoulder when Thea had killed it. Was the spider trying to tell me something? Did Thea know?

The door flew open. Herald burst through, hands held up as if to calm me, but it only made him more threatening. The tips of his fingers glowed violet.

"Dustin, please."

No way out. My friends, hell, my own boss had betrayed me. I'd never done so before, but I knew there was only one option for making my way out of this predicament. I'd have to risk a blind jaunt through the shadows, from inside the building, all the way out to the street.

"Dustin."

I gave Herald one last look and shook my head. I felt hurt, and confused, but more than that, I felt fear, of him, of the Lorica, and of the fate that awaited me if I failed to correctly move through the shadows.

Herald's eyes went wide as I sprinted towards him. I leapt into his shadow, and I stepped.

Chapter 16

I gasped for breath as I rushed out of the darkness, my lungs working like bellows. I lost my footing as I came back to reality, stumbling and sprawling face first into the asphalt. The stinging pain in my arms told me I had skinned them. I sputtered out spit and bits of gravel.

Asphalt. Gravel. The street. I forced my eyes open, straining against the light of lampposts. I had made it outside, alive. My heart clenched as I saw a pair of shoes walk towards, then past me.

"Fucking drunk," the man said. "Pathetic."

He kept walking. I was no longer so selective about how people were treating me that night, nor did I really have the strength to say or do anything back. My standards and tolerance had plunged. As long as someone wasn't out to kill me, they were totally okay in my book.

Then I remembered that I still needed to put as much distance as I could between myself and the Lorica. I was still half a block away, as far as I could tell, at the intersection across the street. I pushed myself to my feet, groaning at the heaviness in my limbs. Fuck. I didn't know that stepping between places I couldn't see would take so much out of me.

My vision was still blurry, and even making it onto the sidewalk was a struggle. I didn't relish the idea of stepping through walls again, but neither did I like the idea of being trapped in the Lorica with whatever horrible shenanigans they had planned for me.

I dragged myself across the street, then down one block, then another. My breath was coming back to me in spurts, but it came in shivers. It was far colder in the Dark Room, and that chill hadn't left my body, haunting my bones with frosted fingers. And in my hurry I'd forgotten to grab a jacket.

No more stepping for a while, that much I knew. I was feeling sick, too, but maybe that was because of the massive dinner I shoveled into my body. But I tried not be so hard on myself. Who knew I was going to be going on the run so soon after anyway?

Yeah, yeah. I know. The entire evening had been a string of terrible decisions, one after the other, but what choice did I really have? I still couldn't understand why the Lorica would want to hide the dagger's existence from me. All I could think was that it made them complicit somehow. I didn't know where else to turn, what else to do, so I made yet another stupid decision for the evening. I went to see my father.

Dad was home. The light in the dining room was on, bright enough for me to see that he was only just picking his way through yet another frozen dinner, far more interested in cracking open the first of the six-pack he'd just pulled out of the fridge.

The tree's trunk felt cool against my back, and I rubbed my elbows in a desperate bid to find some warmth. It was only just working. It would have been better if I didn't have my back up against the tree, I suppose, but I just felt a need to hug the shadows. Just in case.

It was comforting, almost, just watching dad from out in the yard. And yeah, maybe Thea tried to tell me that it wasn't the best thing for me to indulge in, but by that point I wasn't sure I trusted her to know what was best for me anymore.

The bushes by my feet rustled. I frowned, stamping at the ground. Without even having to check I knew that the rats had reached all the way out here, too. When the hell were they going to stop behaving so erratically? Who even knew there were so many rats in the city?

I gazed back at the window and sighed. Not for

the first time I wondered how it might have panned out if I stepped into the living room, or even knocked on the front door. Not for the first time I ran through the many expressions I would see on my father's face when he saw me. All of them involved some mix of terror and revulsion. The dead don't just come back.

The bushes rustled much harder this time. I jumped away, startled, my arms still folded across my chest. Out of the foliage stepped evidence that maybe, just maybe, the dead do return.

It was the man from the other night, the one who chased me down. Correction: it was the vampire, and that entire half of his face that had been charred by sunlight was perfect again, healed to be as handsome and pallid as the uninjured half. I stumbled away, deathly afraid of the reality that I didn't have it in me to escape through the shadows, not so soon after that exertion at the Lorica.

The man raised a hand, almost dismissively, half a greeting, and half reassurance. "Relax. I'm not here to kill you. Not tonight, at least."

I turned from him to the window, and back. Fuck. Now he knew where dad lived. Great job, Dustin. I'd led the vampire right to him.

"Honestly," the vampire said. "We couldn't care less about him. It's you we want."

There was a casual tone to his banter that was somehow close enough to convincing me that he was telling the truth. I kept my hands to myself and cautiously leaned back against the tree, but this time I made a mental note of the fact that Bastion's knife in my pocket could very well be used as a stake, in case of emergency.

I scoffed. "Who is 'we?' Don't tell me you're working for the Lorica, too."

As if. The Lorica might have considered itself the authority on the arcane underground and the Valero that lived behind the Veil, but it didn't seem to have much of an equal opportunity hiring policy when it came to non-humans.

Hell, I didn't even know they existed until a few days ago. Again I wondered why Thea and the others hadn't bothered to brief me about something so basic. They didn't want to overwhelm me with too much information, Prudence said. Hah. A likely story. What else were they hiding from me?

But the vampire scoffed in return. "You and your precious Lorica. No. My boss is different. Better, I'd say, but that's all subjective. He just wants to have a word with you is all."

"The Black Hand."

The vampire cocked an eyebrow. "The black what now? What the hell are you talking about?"

I blinked. It was only natural for him to deny it. "Whoever this is you're working for. They just want to talk. That's it?"

"Yup. Says that he needs to meet you for himself. That you're special." The vampire said "special" with the kind of sneer reserved for when you discovered a worm in your salad by finding half of it still wriggling on your fork. "Can't imagine why. Says you have gifts he could find useful."

I frowned. "I'm not about to work for your kind."

The man laughed. "My kind? And what kind is that?"

I shrugged. "The bad guys." The words sounded stupid to me before they even left my mouth. "The ones who move in darkness."

Again the man chuckled. "Strange sentiments from someone who literally walks in shadows. Fine trick you have there."

"Yeah, well. I'm glad I have it or else you might have actually nailed me that night." This felt awkward, yet correct, somehow, conversing with someone who was planning to suck my blood just nights before. "Where's the other guy, anyway? The hairy one?" Gil. That was his name.

The vampire nodded at the sky. "Full moon."

Oh. So he was a werewolf after all. Great. Just great.

The man slid a pale hand into the pocket of his leather jacket, then retrieved a pack of cigarettes. I didn't know vampires smoked. I realized then that I didn't know a hell of a lot about much of anything. He offered me the pack. I declined by waving a hand.

"Suit yourself," he said, lighting the cigarette

with a clink of his Zippo. I gestured at his lighter, making a face.

"You're not afraid of that?"

"What, a little bit of fire? Come on, man." I watched the ember of his cigarette glow as he took a puff. His skin was flawless in the orange light. I couldn't help myself. I had to know.

"So," I said, pointing at my own face. "That just grew back?"

The vampire raised an eyebrow, clearly annoyed, but making an effort not to show that he was. "Yeah. I had to feed, stay low for a while, but yeah. 'It grew back.' Pssh. Asshole."

I shrugged. "My boss only wanted to help me."

"Yeah, about that. Your boss is kind of a huge bitch. You know that?"

I shrugged again. "You were kind of trying to kill me."

He raised a finger. "Was not. At worst I would have taken, like, a mouthful of blood. But I'm under strict orders not to hurt you."

He scoffed again, then brought the cigarette back to his lips. He blew the smoke in slender curls out of his nostrils, in the way that a kid in high school might do to try and impress someone.

"I was just playing with you," he said, with the nerve to sound hurt. "Was just gonna rough you up a little."

I shook my head. "Not cool."

"If you say so."

I stared at the house for a moment, aware of the dead thing beside me, wondering how it could smoke a cigarette down to a stub without functioning lungs, then deciding that I had a better question to ask.

"Is this weird for you? Talking to me like this. We're supposed to be enemies." I shrugged. "Sort of feels like we're just hanging out."

The man kept his eyes trained on the house. "I'm off the clock. Sue me." He cocked an eyebrow, ventured a look at my face, then turned right back to the window. "What was your name again? I forget. My boss told me, but it's been a minute since that monster you worked for torched my face off."

"What do you need my name for? Gonna use it against me in a spell? I don't think so."

"Dumb-ass. Vampire, remember? I don't do magic. Don't need to." He puffed the last of his cigarette and flicked the filter onto the ground, stubbing it out with the heel of one very expensive-looking sneaker. "Just wanna make sure what to put on your gravestone in case I end up killing you."

I sighed, and in the same exhalation, gave the vampire my name.

"Nice to meet you," the vampire said, without any warmth in his voice. He didn't extend a hand, nor did he give me the benefit of a passing glance. "I'm Sterling."

"Sterling." I chuckled. "As in silver?"

"Oh," Sterling said, cocking his head, his face more expressive than I'd seen all night. "And that's funny why? Because I'm a vampire? Die in a fire. That's racist."

"No, it's not."

"Well, it's prejudiced."

I shrugged.

"It's my name." The vampire called Sterling stuck his hands back into his pockets. "So. Why the hell are we standing outside this garbage pile of a house anyway?"

I felt something prickle at my neck. I only grew up in that garbage pile, after all. Had fun times, even. But this wasn't the time or place to engage the vampire. Sterling, for whatever reason, was being civil, and maybe that was even going to help me somehow. I could put him at ease, wheedle information out of him, or at least wait for him to make a cocky mistake and slip.

"It's my house. Or at least it used to be. That's my dad in there."

"And you're standing out here, because?"

"I'm supposed to be dead. Long story. Can't just walk in there."

Sterling sniffed. "You should go to him, you know."

"I can't. I just said so."

"Look," Sterling said, eyes turned to cold steel. "Whatever it is that happened between you, it can't be so bad that he'd be upset to see his son walk into his house. He'll be surprised, sure, but if your father ever loved you, give him a minute and he'll be happier than you know. That's how family works."

"You're a vampire. What the hell do you know about family?"

"Plenty. Everyone I used to love, everyone I used to know is dead. That's what I know." He kicked at the grass. "Go to him."

The leaves shuffled, and the vampire was gone, but the echo of his voice remained.

"Go to him."

I couldn't. I didn't.

Chapter 17

I could have skipped town. That was always an option. I could have gone somewhere smaller and quieter, or headed upstate to blend in with the weirdoes in San Francisco. Of course, I wouldn't have been enthusiastic about it, but the clever thing to do would have been to leave California entirely. Not my favorite option, but hey, beggars can't be choosers, right?

And that was assuming Romira or one of the other Eyes didn't sell me out. I never bothered asking how far the Eyes could see, but I wanted to think that I could at least count on Romira. But then I remembered. That was how I used to feel about Thea, and Herald, for that matter. I shoved those thoughts away. It all still stung too much.

For now, I needed to focus on packing and grabbing as much of my shit as I needed to make it out on the road. I already had most of my essentials from the duffle bag I brought with me to HQ, but the apartment still had some of my valuables in it, so that's where I went.

Stop. I know what you're thinking. But there was no way I was leaving without those last few remnants of my previous life that I managed to salvage, the bundle of letters I stole back from my roommates, the rare pictures of me as a kid. They mattered. They bonded me to who I was, reminded me that I was a person before I died, before someone drove a wedge between the lives I led before and after the knife pierced my heart.

I knew I had no reason to believe him, but there was something almost honorable in how forthright Sterling was with me, how he specifically said that he was ordered not to hurt me – and how he still had an urge to feed on my blood. It creeped me the fuck out, not gonna lie, but I was relieved when he told me that I was safe from his bizarre demon-worshipping, bronze mask-wearing death cult, if only for one night.

And I wanted my jacket back, too. That was the very first priority after I was killed. I went all the way back to that shitty apartment I rented with my shitty roommates just to retrieve the thing, this ratty old sucker that by rights should have fallen apart ages ago. But it still fit, and it had worn its way to this comforting softness.

Back when I still lived with my dad he threatened to throw it out all the time, and that became a running joke. He would never have done that, not when he was responsible for stitching every little rip, for patching over its holes. That jacket, that's who I was. And that's who I still am.

It was right where I'd left it in the apartment, slung over the back of a chair from the night when I'd discovered the Pruitts. I picked up the jacket, feeling its familiar textures and mended tears under the pads of my fingers. It was hard to believe how quickly things had changed, between finding out about the entities, and now this revelation about the dagger.

I sighed, only wishing that things didn't have to end this way. I might not ever get the answers I needed, about what happened that night someone shoved cold metal into my chest, but maybe those answers didn't matter anymore. Maybe it was time to move on.

Before leaving, I made one last sweep of the apartment, just to check that I hadn't left anything behind. It smarted a little knowing that I was forced to leave something I couldn't ever take with me regardless. But dad was going to be fine. Whatever the Lorica wanted, it was with me and the things I could do, not with a man whose grief was slowly dragging him into darkness. They wouldn't touch him. At least that's what I told myself. That's what I needed to believe.

Some day, when I learned more about magic, on my own terms, I would find a way to reconnect with my father. As for how that would happen, exactly, would be up to future-Dustin to decide. Maybe someone would help me with a spell to make him forget that I was ever dead, and we could just pick up where we left off. Maybe I could use some kind of magical disguise to ease him into it. Anything that wouldn't traumatize him, any way that could help me get back one precious sliver of the family I used to have.

Right. That was it, then. I started shutting the lights off, one by one, this heavy feeling in the pit of my stomach. It was tough realizing that I was doing exactly what Hecate had warned me against: running, again. But what choice did I have? I couldn't fight the Lorica. Who was I against the combined might of the country's greatest sorcerers?

I clicked off the final light, sighing in resignation, the sound of my breath the only thing left in the apartment – which was why it jolted me when I heard something else.

"Sterling told me you would be here."

I whirled around, my hand flying to the knife in my pocket as I looked for the source of the voice. I didn't have to look very far. The man was only a few feet away from me, the only thing separating us a scant measure of floor. He stood by the window, the tan of his skin visible in the light of the moon, slick, styled hair falling in locks over his shoulders, his beard carefully trimmed. The man wore a fine suit, and a soft leather glove on one hand. On his fingers gleamed gold rings embedded with jewels in amber, orange, and ocher. And his eyes, most striking of all, were yellow, like a cat. Like a beast of prey.

"I don't want any trouble," I said, holding one hand out between us. "I've had enough weirdness this week."

The man stepped forward, his movement so lackadaisical that it was hard to find it threatening, and he spread his arms. "I'm just here to talk."

About what? The god murders? My own death? There were so many variables at play now that it was nothing short of exasperating trying to fit the pieces of the puzzle together. But this, at least, I could figure out on the spot.

"You're Sterling's boss. Whoever you are."

The man tapped the side of his nose, aquiline and handsome, his grin confident. "The very same," he said.

"He promised me that no harm would come to me tonight," I said, willing hardness into my voice, summoning the last dregs of my flagging confidence. "He said he was ordered not to hurt me."

He pressed his hands together, holding them in front of him with the fingers laced, like this was just some business meeting, and not some prolonged threat.

"That was what I ordered him to do, correct. But I made no such promises myself."

I pulled the knife out of my pocket. The man's eyes widened slightly at the sight of it, and he chuckled.

"Let's not be so crude, Dustin. I'm only teasing. Surely Sterling told you that I only wanted to talk."

I frowned. "How do you even know my name? How do you even know about me?"

"And the special things that you can do. How indeed." He ran a finger along the length of the rickety wooden thing I called a dinner table, then inspected the tip of it for dust. "When you died – and I do apologize for bringing up such a stinging memory – your gifts awakened inside of you. Such a stressful, terrible moment for it to happen, but there we are. Magic came alive inside of Dustin Graves on that night, setting aflame. And those of us who perceive magic, those of us who live it, we can see that fire from afar."

I looked around uneasily, only taking some small comfort in the fact that my entire apartment was, at this point, one giant shadow. I was only afraid that I still didn't have the strength to make another shadowstep.

"So that's how the Lorica found me? Is that what you're saying? Because I was some giant beacon when I died – when I awakened?"

The man nodded. "It was such an interesting

signature, too. Not quite like the norm. Imagine that you are only accustomed to seeing orange fire, which, silly me, is how you have experienced fire your whole life anyway. And one night, a black fire appears. It is curious, and it draws many of us."

"So it's not just you and the Lorica who are after me."

"That I know of. You are – different, to say the least, Dustin. May I call you Dustin? You may call me Carver." He smiled tightly, then went on. It was a formality, I knew, and he didn't wait for a response, just went on speaking. "Who knows how many parties are interested in what you can do, and who knows what lengths they'll go to find and, shall we say, acquire you. It's only a shame that you awakened in such unusual, such excruciating circumstances."

"What do you mean?" The hand I was holding the knife with was lowering, like the fight was going out of me. I knew something bad was coming.

"You didn't know?" Carver tutted. "When one awakens to magic is not accurately documented. All we know is that it happens eventually, whether in childhood, adolescence, or even in middle age. Your experience was accelerated because of what happened to you. Your awakening was not an accident. Someone meant to do that to you."

"I – I don't understand."

The man sighed, though not to express impatience. It sounded sad, almost. Sympathetic. "Every mage has a spark inside of them, one that grows into a roaring fire when they come into their power. Whoever did this to you threw kindling on yours by thrusting you into a horrific situation. They forced you to awaken."

"Then my murder had a purpose." I looked at the knife in my hand, my grasp around it now loose, my fingers limp. But I tightened my grip again, my blood going hot. "You had something to do with this."

Carver's eyes flashed. "Don't be foolish."

"You're part of the Black Hand." I pointed at his leather glove. "Hell, you are the Black Hand."

He spoke slowly, incredulous. "The Black Hand."

"That's right. You sacrifice people to your dark gods. No, not just earth entities. You psychos worship the Eldest, don't you?"

It was bait. I didn't have the slightest idea what worshipping them entailed, or how insane someone would have to be to try, but if he knew what the Eldest were –

"Don't you speak of the Eldest so lightly," Carver sneered. Ah. So he did know. "Those things existed before any of us did, even before the gods of myth. They reach everywhere. They hear everything. They see all."

"You seem to know so much about them." I admit, I was more than a little smug that my gambit had gotten him to spill. "So you do worship the Eldest." It was him, then, him and Sterling and Gil, and all those other men in bronze masks. They were my murderers.

"You need to stop speaking of things you do not understand. Who in their right mind would worship the primal forces of madness, chaos, death? I'm sure I don't know what you're talking about, Mr. Graves." He ventured a step forward. "And I'm sure you don't, either."

I raised the knife again, woefully aware that it wouldn't be much help against Carver, whatever he was.

"Oh, I know all right. You're just like that servant of yours. A vampire. You saw what happened to him. All I have to do is tell my mentor." I reached for the gem dangling from my neck, deliberately not touching it with my fingers, aware that I couldn't call on Thea's help again. I prayed that he would call my bluff. "She'll send more sunlight to burn your vampire ass."

Carver's laugh was smooth, like whispers of warm desert wind, like sand tumbling across dunes. "Me, a vampire? No. I'm different. Older. More powerful." He sent his gloved hand out, reaching for my pendant. "Let's just eliminate this nuisance, shall we? It's only getting in the way."

In a panic, I scrambled away, backing up against the last few inches of space I had to retreat into, then hurling the knife as hard as I could. I watched as it streaked towards Carver's throat, the tip of it glinting in the moonlight. He held up one hand, fingers outstretched, then closed it into a fist. In midair the knife shattered into a puff of harmless metal shavings, a cloud of glittering dust.

I gaped. "Well fuck."

Carver cracked his knuckles. "Indeed."

My hands groped at my body of their own accord, desperately seeking anything else to use as a weapon. I cringed when I patted at my pockets and felt my cellphone – just something else for Carver to obliterate – but my fingers probed in my jacket and found something else. It was tiny, cold, glassy: the bottle of lightning that I'd used to kill the power at the Pruitt mansion.

Carver beckoned. "Give me the pendant, Mr. Graves. No one needs to be hurt tonight."

"You and your people tried to kill me once, and that didn't work. You just came to finish the job. Sorry. Can't let you."

I threw the bottle at Carver, harder than I'd thrown the knife. Maybe it would hit him before he had time to react. His eyes did widen in surprise at the sight of it, but that was quickly overtaken by a look of boredom.

He raised his hand again, the gemstones on his rings glowing, then clenched his fingers into a fist. The bottle disintegrated into a sparkling mist of razor dust – but the lightning needed a place to go, and his body was the closest thing.

Carver's screams curdled my blood. The room lit up as his entire body became a beacon for all the electricity that had been stored inside the crystal phial. The tiny box of my apartment filled with the smell of cooking flesh. I didn't dare look at Carver's face, and maybe I felt a momentary swell of pity for how painful his death had to be, but this man – he had tried to kill me. An eye for an eye. I ran for the door and threw it open.

And while the sound of sizzling didn't cease, the smell of burning hair and meat still wafting through the room, Carver had stopped screaming. I was almost tempted to turn and look if he really was dead, but I didn't have to – he spoke.

"Feisty," he groaned. Outside in the hall shouts and footsteps thundered, the neighbors alarmed by his screams. I didn't know why I bothered, but I dared to look him in the face. I really shouldn't have.

Carver's skin, whatever was exposed of it, was a burnt, molten mass of disrepair, his left eye fused shut, his cheek a slurry that looked likely to run right off his jaw, his mouth a ragged, pulped mess. I bit my tongue, fighting the urge to vomit right there.

He shouldn't have survived that. Carver, whatever he was, couldn't possibly have been alive. I zipped up my jacket, slung my backpack over my shoulder, and turned to run.

"Graves," Carver burbled from the remains of

his mouth. Something in his voice, a bizarre, distant authority in spite of his ruination, made me stop long enough to listen. "Why are you so afraid of what you are? Come to me if you want true knowledge. Come to me if you want true power. Come to me if you want the truth."

Chapter 18

My heart pounded against my chest. Had I been wrong all along? The Lorica really did want to help me, and that thing with the dagger, it was all a misunderstanding. Wasn't it? My brain pounded in time with my heart, one threatening to explode out of my skull, the other from my chest.

What else was I supposed to do? Who else could I go to for help? The police? Hah. The thought of Carver disintegrating bullets in midair, or a gun out of someone's hands – hell, he could probably do it to people, too, turn them into fine mists of blood.

Besides, the Lorica hadn't sent anyone to hound me yet. Didn't that mean something? That they knew I was coming back, that things were going to be okay? I hurried onward down the block, looking over my shoulder for any sign of Sterling, Gil, or worse, Carver.

God knew what Carver was, but I had a horrible feeling that it wasn't going to take him long to reconstitute and come after me. It was him, then, the Black Hand. I should have known all along, and I should have known that Sterling was lying about not harming me. And now he knew where dad lived, too. Awesome. Great job, Dust.

Finally, the Lorica building loomed into sight, its silhouette in the gloom squat and misshapen, but just then it was heartening, like a fortress from another time. Safety, I thought, or something like it. I held onto my backpack, focused on a patch of darkness on the asphalt, and shadowstepped.

It was cold and creepy as always, in the Dark Room, but it was still a damn sight better than trying to bypass the security system. I needed to talk to someone, and fast. Herald, but that would take too much explaining for why I ran out in the first place. It would have to be Thea. Did she even stay this late? Should I have contacted her via gemstone first?

Not that it mattered anymore. My feet hit wooden flooring as I emerged from the shadows. I didn't spot anyone in the Lorica when I arrived, or no one who mattered, anyway, the lower level filled with the quiet murmur of grunts pushing paper. I made a beeline for Thea's office, throwing the door open and dashing in.

"Thea."

She made no motion and didn't seem at all surprised by my frenetic entrance, keeping her back to me as she gazed through her windows. I always did find it strange, how internally, Thea's office was only on the second floor, yet it still afforded her a view of the city as if we were twenty stories up. Whatever she was looking at had her fullest attention.

"Thea?"

She finally acknowledged my presence, turning her head slightly over her shoulder. "You're back, Graves. I was worried when Herald told me you'd burst out of here." She faced me, a small smile spreading across her lips. "And it seems you're content to burst in just as suddenly as you'd left."

My breathing slowed as I composed myself, and I put some semblance of rigidity into my posture. The urgency was still coursing through my blood, but I knew instinctively that just babbling everything at Thea at top speed wouldn't help my case.

"The Black Hand," I said. "They came for me again. This time it was their leader. At least I think it was."

Thea raised an eyebrow, like she was having a hard time following what I meant. "Oh. Of course. The Black Hand." She cleared her throat and tutted. "See, this is what comes of mistrusting those who only want to help you." Her words cut at me, but her expression was soft, almost kind.

"I. I wasn't thinking. I didn't know what I was doing."

Thea smiled. "Yes, that seems to be a theme for you, Mr. Graves. But you did well to come directly to me. Darker elements are trying to seduce you, when I'm the one that you should be trusting. This Black Hand character. Did he offer you anything?"

What a strange thing to ask, I thought. Shouldn't she have been more concerned about him trying to attack me?

"Truth," I said carefully. "He offered me the truth."

"Deception," Thea said, shaking her head. "They've moved past attempting to murder you. Now it's indoctrination that they'll pursue. You're more useful to them that way. And worse still that they have someone working on the inside to help them." She pulled something out of her pocket, placing the familiar, spiny sharpness of it on her glass desk.

I stared at the dagger, than back up at her. "Herald? You don't mean that. He can't be working with them." Couldn't he? Just an hour ago I'd almost believed that Herald and Thea — no, that the entire Lorica was in league against me. My fingers ran through my hair of their own accord, tugging in confusion.

"We have good reason to believe it was him," Thea said, her voice a mix of resignation and cold accusation. "He's working with the Black Hand. Or are you trying to convince me that he's innocent?" She took a single step, and that smallest movement filled the room with her presence: sharp, brilliant, suffocating. "Perhaps the man you met convinced you. Have you decided to trust your murderers so easily?"

"You know that isn't true. Herald is innocent. Where is he?"

"He's safe," Thea said, in a way that told me he wasn't. "For the moment. The Lorica has ways of handling internal matters that will ensure this sort of thing doesn't happen again." She took another step forward, close enough that she could lay a hand on my shoulder. Thea squeezed, the gems on one hand glinting as she did, and it was almost comforting.

"You're cleverer than that, Dustin. I knew why you ran. You saw the knife, and you knew immediately, didn't you? I always pegged you for your intelligence, your keenness. Surely you know it was him. It was so clever of the Black Hand to get such an innocuous-looking plant, too, someone so inoffensive. So harmless."

"No," I said. "Someone planted the blade on him. Herald isn't tied to the Black Hand, nor to the god murders. I know it."

Thea watched me, her face a mix of interest,

and pity. For a moment, all was silence in her office, apart from the quiet, low hum of her computer, and from somewhere else, perhaps within the walls, a quiet, low chittering. The rats. Always the rats.

"You know that you can trust me, don't you, Dustin? I would never wish you harm. You're far too important to me."

I looked up at her, wondering what to believe. "To the Lorica, you mean."

She smiled sadly, and shook her head. "To me, Dustin. I've told you before. You're a special person. I would almost say irreplaceable."

"I don't understand," I began to say, my thoughts left unspoken, when a commotion streamed in from the hallway outside.

"Dustin," a voice shouted. Prudence?

"Where the hell are you?" And Bastion?

The door exploded off its hinges, splinters spraying across the immaculate white of Thea's carpet. Bastion strode in, face like thunder, his hand held menacingly up in front of him. Prudence rushed in after, her fists already charged with blue fire.

"Bastion? What's going on?"

Prudence bent forward and yelled. "Get away from her, Dustin!"

On instinct my feet backed away, but I didn't make it very far. Thea's fingers were locked around my wrist, clamping with an alarming strength.

"Thea? You're hurting me. I – "

The air whizzed as the dagger flew between us, carving a quick, shallow crescent and slicing into my cheek. A warm wetness welled up against my skin. The pain was brief, immediate. The betrayal hurt more. Thea watched impassively as she unclenched her hand, leaving me free to stumble away.

"Thea?" I clutched at my cheek, alarmed at the stickiness oozing down my face. "What. Why?"

A powerful force gripped me and pulled me bodily away from her, my heels dragging against the carpet as I went. I turned, ready to fight Bastion off my back, when I realized that he was still at the door, grabbing me with the force of his power.

"Idiot," he snarled. "You heard me and Prue. We said to get away."

Thea seemed distracted, staring at the point of the dagger, angling it carefully so that whatever she'd drawn of my blood stayed along its blade, smiling to herself as she balanced the droplet of fluid, so bright red against the dagger's edge.

"Herald alerted us," Prudence said. "He said that you'd taken off, and he told Thea you disappeared. By the time Bastion and I made it to HQ, Herald had been taken into the Lorica's custody."

"So disobedient," Thea said absentmindedly, her eyes still focused on the dagger. "So inefficient. I was upset that Herald allowed you to escape, so I had him punished. I've been working here forever. My word is gold. The Hands sprang into action and restrained him as soon as I asked. I didn't need him after all. Just the dagger. And you, Dustin."

"What have you done to him?" I shouted.

"He's safe," Bastion said, tugging on my arm. "She wanted all of HQ distracted so she could grab the dagger and finish what she started."

"And finish I will. Look how Dustin ran so quickly from his friends, only to come crawling back when he couldn't find the answers he wanted. Oh, I could have found the dagger myself, truthfully. Or I could have kept it after I stabbed you in the heart."

My scar ached. "It was you. The cultist in the bronze mask. The one who murdered me."

"Murdered?" Thea scoffed. I watched as she held her palm under the dagger, to make sure she could catch my blood if it threatened to drip off the blade. I watched the way she handled the dagger with skill, with painful familiarity. "I gave you a new life. Security. Power. I gave you purpose."

"You planted the Book of Plagues on the Pruitts. You killed Resheph and Lei Kung. It was you."

"Poor Dustin. Sweet Dustin. About time you figured it out. It took the Hounds forever to find the dagger, too. I had to plant it somewhere, after all, erase all traces of it being tied to me."

"You pinned this all on Herald," I said. Something stirred in my stomach. I had blamed him myself.

"In retrospect, it might have been amusing to send you to find the dagger. There would have been something so poetic and bittersweet about setting you to fetch your own murder weapon, like the good little dog that you are." Her smile grew wider. "It wouldn't have been hard to convince you, not with that collar around your neck."

My fingers flew to my pendant. It was cold now, even against my skin. "What?"

She laughed. "I need you to keep wearing that," she said, and almost immediately a sense of comfort, of warmth washed across my skin. "I need you to trust me."

The gem was manipulating me, somehow. She was controlling me through it. I gritted my teeth and ripped it off my neck, the leather thong snapping.

"How dare you. I trusted you, Thea."

Prudence reached for the gem, snatching it out of my fingers. "We all did, Dustin," she said grimly, clenching her fingers, crushing the opal into powder.

Thea only smiled. "You know what's curious about my gemstones? They only just work on humans. Slightest suggestions, little nudges, that's the best I can do. On less intelligent creatures, however, they work wonders." She stretched out her fingers, admiring her rings, the opals that glistened there. "Rodents, for example."

"Why, Thea?" Prudence said. I couldn't tell if she was just buying time, but something in the way that she and Bastion hadn't advanced told me that we needed to be very, very careful about handling this.

"The thing about rats," Thea said, "is that they can get around very quickly. Unseen, agile. And they're everywhere, too. Slaying Resheph gave me dominion over the vermin, but it was my gems that gave me total control. And you know, it's remarkable what you can do with a horde of rats. Their tiny little claws are perfect for marking things, for scratching things out. A design, for example." She smiled. "Or a circle."

Bastion elbowed his way past me. "Fuck," he muttered, holding out one hand. "She cast a circle. That's why she needed the rats."

"Well done, Sebastion." Thea laughed. "You were never the cleverest, but you certainly are quick in your own way." She ran her finger along the edge of the dagger, smearing my blood across the blade, muttering softly. My stomach turned.

"No," I shouted, rushing forward. "Stop. What are you doing?"

Her chanting ended. "Closing the circle."

Thea fell to one knee and thrust the dagger into the ground. The world exploded into white, a silvery brilliance bursting from lines that radiated in spokes from where the dagger struck. I held my hands up to my eyes as the energy surged its way out of Thea's office, as massive pillars of blistering light detonated out of the very earth all across the city.

The rats. Valero. Thea had inscribed the entire city into a gargantuan circle.

Chapter 19

My feet tangled as Bastion, Prudence, and I ran for the exit. HQ was in chaos, the entirety of the building blaring with the end-song of invisible klaxons. Thea was nowhere to be found, but her shattered office windows gave us a good guess. That's why we were headed for the streets.

Everything was a whirl. The woman I thought to trust the most was the one who had literally stabbed me through my heart. I felt at my cheek, at the crusted gore drying against the cut Thea had left there. All this while she had played me with her opal, biding her time with casting a circle over the entirety of the city. What kind of madness had driven her to this, and what kind of madness had she brought down on Valero? I clenched my fists, dreading those very answers as

I rushed out onto the street with the rest of the Lorica.

The city had transformed into a terrifying mockery of the day, enormous pillars of light illuminating Valero with a frigid, horrible white, the absence of color so bleak against the urban landscape, an ivory inferno.

Fuck the underground, am I right? Forget the Veil. People were pouring out into the streets, panicking – normals, most of them, pointing at the light beaming into the clouds. They clapped their hands over their ears at the horrible keening noise that sounded like distant laughter, or screaming, laced with the awful, discordant music that seemed to echo from the very sky itself. And all around us the wind lashed, thunder rumbling, the warped aftershocks of the storm god's passing. Was it the end of the world? Was that what Thea had triggered?

"Get everyone to safety," Prudence shouted over the din, directing what little staff we had on hand to usher the normals out and away from Central Square. Hands, Hounds, Wings alike rushed to help, and still I had a sinking feeling. What could the Lorica do for them? I saw Scions mixed in among the crowd, some muttering to themselves, preparing spells, and others barking orders. But again: to what avail?

People stood at the doors and balconies of their apartments, children clutched at their waists. Far down the streets sirens blared, though not loud enough to truly be heard over the alien song of the circle. Lights that should have flashed red and blue pulsed as emergency vehicles rushed in all directions, but their colors were washed over by the all-encompassing white.

Then the droves began, a mass exodus of people streaming out of the square, out of restaurants, out of hotels and homes, cars choking the streets as the normals headed – where, exactly? Movement went in all directions, but there was no clear sign of haven, of any sort of safety. Six massive pillars encircled the city. Who knew if they formed a barrier between Valero and the world outside?

Chaos. That was what Thea had initiated, and if that was all she wanted, she had it. But I knew it wasn't the end of things. Valero had been twisted into a nightmarish alabaster hellscape, yet it was only the setting of the stage. This was just the beginning.

Worse, still, was what Thea had become.

She was suspended, somehow, far above the power lines, rotating slowly, as if she were surveying the city, watching her handiwork. There was a different quality to her, the luminosity glowing from inside her skin as if she had become a living lamp, a pale firefly. She stretched out her arms, her hands reaching to either side of her, the rings on her fingers now grown into orbs of spectacular luminescence, each gemstone glowing like a sphere of light.

Thea threw her head back, as if breathing in the night air, savoring her newfound form and power. She turned to face us, her meditation complete. Her eyes, in contrast to her body, were pits of total darkness, deep and devoid of emotion, apart from glee. When she smiled, more light poured out of her mouth. Looking upon her was painful, like staring into the sun. She was beautiful, radiant, terrible.

"Hang back," Bastion said from somewhere beside me. "Let her make the first move."

Like I needed to be told. I stood with the others, some thirty of us who had poured out of the Lorica, all of us unsure of what we were meant to do. Odessa was with us, her expression flat, her body deathly still. Even the Scions were playing things cautiously.

But someone broke away from our pack. One of the Hands, a man I didn't know all too well. Jonas, I think. He went straight for Thea, his hand cupped around a wad of fire, running blindly for her in some foolish, brazen attempt to be a hero.

"Jonas," someone shouted. "Don't!"

It was hard to tell where Thea was looking, or if she was looking at all, but it happened so seamlessly. She reached one hand to her side, calling glimmers of light to gather in her palm and between her fingers. I knew what was coming. Thea had used her power on me, once, to create arcane grenades made of explosive radiance, testing my talent by bombarding me with spheres of light as deadly as fireballs. I recognized the shapes she was forming this time. I should have known.

The light in her hand gathered and solidified into a lance even taller than she was. Then another spear manifested, and another, until six of them hovered in the air around her. Another shout of warning rang across the square, but Jonas kept charging. He thrust his hand upward, lobbing the ball of flame. The corner of Thea's mouth quirked. She opened her hand, fingers outstretched, and all six spears launched in concert, sailing unerringly for the ground.

The spears met the fireball in midair, snuffing it out through sheer force, then kept flying. All six impaled Jonas at once, slamming with enough force to crater the asphalt in a burst of blood and broken gravel. His body went rigid, then all at once limp, supported only by the spears.

Thea clenched her fist, and the spears disappeared. Jonas slumped to the ground, bleeding from six massive holes – just like the Pruitts, like Resheph. Someone screamed.

"Everyone stay back," Bastion roared. No one needed to be told this time.

"You should listen to him," Thea said. Her speech had a different quality, like it was coming from a place far away, threaded over and under with echoes that might have been copies of her own voice, or the sound of something entirely other, alien. She looked over her shoulder, spinning on her invisible axis again, admiring the pillars of light. "Let the circle do its work."

I looked back, watching for the Scions, noting that several of them were still mouthing words, weaving their spells. Complex, destructive ones, I hoped, spells that could end this horror quickly. Maybe that was how I could help, I thought. Buy them time. Be the diversion.

"Why did you do all this, Thea?" I shouted. "Killing the Pruitts, the god murders. Killing me. Why?"

Thea swiveled again, her black eyes settling on me. "Terrible, wasn't it?" She hovered lower, closer. The shuffle of activity around me told me that the others were clearing off in fear, that perhaps I should as well. But I had a job to do. "I do apologize."

"For what?" My teeth ground into each other so much it hurt. "For everything you've done? For all the lives you've taken?"

Thea tilted her head, thinking. "I suppose. And for deceiving you, and the Lorica. I needed time, you know, to get everything in order, to lay my plans out. It was so simple, too. Who would ever suspect anything so serious from rats? If I had slain a greater entity, there would have been more cause to question and investigate. As I expected, no one was too concerned with the death of a minor deity."

"That's what you wanted everyone to think,"

Prudence said. She seemed to have the same idea: let Thea gloat like the big damn villain she thought she was. The difference was that I really did want answers.

"But the rats. Oh, the rats. Such simple creatures. It didn't take much out of me, you know, to control them, to get their claws to leave little marks across the city. Make enough marks –"

"Enough to draw a circle," Prudence said.

Thea smiled, holding her hands out, spinning in place like a triumphant child.

"And what's the circle for, Thea? Are you planning to destroy Valero?"

Thea stopped spinning. "You'll find out soon enough. You're so clever and all."

"Not as clever as you," I spat, the taste in my mouth bitter. "You set me to find you. You were the murderer, and you wanted me to find you."

"And you failed, until it was too late. Not quite the best Hound at the Lorica, then." That stung more than it should have. Why, I couldn't say. Maybe I even believed her all those times she praised me. "But I can't say that you were ever a bad dog, Dustin. You always wore the collar I gave you, like a good little puppy."

I reached at my throat for the gem that was no longer there. "You used me," I said.

"How melodramatic. Putting you on the altar, though? Turning you into a sacrifice? Now that was using you."

My nails dug into the palms of my hands.

"That blade was never meant to kill you, Dustin. It was only meant to plant something inside of your heart."

I staggered, clutching at my scar. I looked down at myself, at the back of my hands, then up at her again. Is that why it hurt all those times? Or was Thea bluffing again?

Her smile went wider, the black of her eyes gleaming. "Then you know, don't you? Do you feel it even now, growing inside you like a cancer? And now that you've ripened, now that something as powerful as Hecate has granted you her favor, your blood has sweetened, perfect for closing a circle as grand and majestic as this. You've served your purpose, Dustin, and in time, you may have other roles to fulfill."

She always spoke in puzzles, but this was the only time her obtuseness ever truly frustrated me. I groped at my chest, feeling for my scar, for my heartbeat. What was growing inside me? What other purpose could I possibly have?

"You killed me," I said. "You took everything away from me. My father. My life."

Her smile turned piteous. "Which never really amounted to much, Dustin. You said so yourself."

More hushed whispers came from behind me, the Scions still at work. I had planned to buy them time at first, but now I was angry.

"Why me? At least tell me that. Why did you plant your filth in me? What made me so special?"

Thea folded her hands together, hovering even closer to the ground so that she was barely feet away.

"You aren't special at all, Dustin Graves. There was nothing deliberate about your selection. You were just – an accident."

An accident. All those times Thea said I was worth something, I'd believed her.

Then the noise of the pillars, the jet engine clamor, even the rumbling of the storm all came to an abrupt stop. Thea whipped about, her ears pricking up at the silence.

From somewhere behind me, Bastion gasped. "What – what's happening now?"

Thea spoke softly. "It has begun."

Each of the six pillars around the city shot into the sky, meeting in the clouds and coalescing into a sphere far above us. The ball stilled, for a second, then unleashed a singular beam of illumination that fell shrieking back to earth, a half mile away. Backlit by the massive shaft of light, Thea looked like a goddess herself. A demon. An entity.

"This I do for the glory of the greatest of all beings, for those who came before the others, before us all. For the Old Ones. For the first among them, and the last among us, who shall survive when the sun dies and the stars wink out."

The pillar wavered. A black spot at its heart

began to grow, tearing larger and larger, like a hole in reality. It was a gateway. The wailing, the screaming, the cacophony of alien music built to a piercing pitch.

Thea smiled. "This I do for the memory of my children." And from the rift probed a single tentacle. "This I do for the very Eldest."

Chapter 20

The keening began again. The gap in reality widened ever larger as an unspeakable noise poured out of it, a clamor of shrieking metal, discordant music, of inhuman voices chattering and muttering. Thea floated higher above the ground, her hands clasped together as she watched the rift expectantly, a beatific smile on her face.

Then all at once, the screeching stopped.

Another tentacle curled out of the gateway, then another, and another, probing and feeling at nothing, so many glistening, black tendrils. They were covered in slime, as if the nether hell from which they were birthed was drenched in this matter, some infernal amniotic fluid.

The first of the black things stepped through

the portal, and my heart fell through my stomach. The screaming began anew, but this time, it came from the people all around us.

The creature was like nothing I had ever seen. It was only the basest caricature of something humanoid, a mockery of life, pawing with its talons at the air, as if discovering the world for the very first time. Spindly black legs propelled it forward, with all the twitching, excitable discovery of a child learning to walk.

And it had no head. Where its neck should have been sprouted a nest of tentacles, an innumerable mass of them in various lengths and thicknesses, lashing and whipping at the air. And with a scream that came from some unseen mouth, the thing staggered, jerked forward, then broke into a run.

Two, three more of its brethren, then a dozen more poured out of the slit in reality. The alien horrors raced forward, their movements more feral than human, loping along on two legs or four, or all of their tentacles as they saw fit. They hurtled and howled, a gleaming, wriggling mass of leather-black standing out sickeningly against the city's artificial pallor, like nightmarish drawings come to life.

A brilliant heat pulsed behind me, and instinctively I ducked as I turned to look. Romira – good old Romira from reception – had conjured a fireball the size of a truck, and with a spirited shout, sent it streaking towards the mass of abominations. It collided with them in a burst of crimson flame, and the tentacled creatures flailed horribly, ululating and gurgling, the smell of them like burnt rubber and human hair.

The flames ate at the squirming, screaming beasts as if they were kindling, and I felt a momentary swell of relief. But Thea was looking smug. The rift was still humming, screeching, and I knew that more of those creatures would come pouring out of the gap. Romira was standing off to the side, clutching at her chest, wheezing. Casting the fire must have taken a lot out of her.

There was no doubting the incredible feats of power mages were capable of, but we were still human after all. Once enough of these things came stumbling out and our Hands ran low on power, I knew they would overrun the city. And like clockwork, as if in answer, more of the monsters came screaming out of the portal, howling from mouths I couldn't see.

But then I did see, and I regretted everything. I glimpsed their true mouths, the slits at the tips of their tentacles, hidden in the palms of their hands, all lined with points of yellowed teeth. What kind of mad god would create these abominations?

No time to think. They were closing in, and fast, rushing straight for the ranks of the Lorica, as if they knew instinctively to attack us first. The Hands launched into battle, bursts of light flashing from across the square as they deployed their spells.

Here, a crackle and sizzle as a bolt of lightning leapt in a chain, frying a dozen of the creatures to a crisp and leaving them in tangled, molten heaps. There, a woman shouted as she thrust her palms out, slick icicles the size of kitchen knives firing from her hands in a terrifying salvo of deadly frost.

And me, I huddled towards the back of the line, unsure of what the hell I could even begin to do to help.

"Hang back," Prudence said, her hand across my chest, as if sensing my hesitation. She flew into action. Blazing blue energy wreathed her fists and her feet, and with every strike she obliterated another abomination with unflinching brutality. A single punch blew a hole through one creature's chest, and a kick severed another's body at the waist through sheer, devastating force.

Before I could even thank her a single black tentacle sailed into view. One of the things had come upon me somehow, its dozens of teeth clicking as it jerked ever closer, an alien chittering issuing from its many mouths. My heart leapt to my throat, and I eyed the monster's shadow, ready to step.

It burst into a hundred pieces, tentacles falling to the concrete in limp tatters, its insides spattering the asphalt. I held my hand up against it, grimacing as cold, black blood splashed against the back of my arm.

"Graves!" Bastion shouted. "She said to hang back. Listen."

"I – thanks," I muttered, unsure that he could even hear me. I knew it didn't matter anymore, watching as he held his hand out, as stray rocks and debris from the street lifted at his command. On their own, they were just pebbles, but under Bastion's power, everything became a weapon. He spread his fingers and the rubble shot forth, spraying at the oncoming horrors, ripping them apart like a hail of bullets.

Stumbling backwards, letting the fighters surge ahead of me, I wondered how long Bastion or any of the Hands could keep this up. There was no stemming the endless tide spilling from the rift. And somehow, things went from bad to worse. Sensing that there were enough of their brethren to keep the Lorica occupied, the newest batch of creatures from the portal broke away from the procession and flooded into the square, clearly meaning to spread throughout the city.

"No," I shouted, amid screams of warning and horror from around me, from all the others who had spotted the stragglers. From somewhere above us, Thea was laughing to herself, triumphant. She hadn't even joined the fray, I realized, saving her energies for whatever dark, unknowable purpose. This was bad. She was getting what she wanted: a bloodbath on the scale of an entire city, a grisly offering for her chthonic masters.

Then a cold, commanding voice rang out to drown out all the others.

"Stop."

It was Odessa, the Scion I had met at Thea's office. Heads turned at the sound of her voice, and I watched as she lifted a single delicate hand to the sky. Threads of light emanated from each of her fingers, drifting lazily into the clouds as they wove themselves into a translucent sphere that covered the very extent of the square. She was conjuring a dome, a massive, transparent field meant, I began to understand, to keep the abominations from breaking out into the city.

But it was also meant to keep the innocents out. By the Lorica's definition I knew that it also meant the peacekeepers. Responders had only now reached Central Square, but all around the perimeter of the dome, squad cars and ambulances were parked helplessly, unable to penetrate Odessa's field. A few officers fired into the shield, attempting to shatter it. I watched, open mouthed as they were, as the bullets simply disappeared.

Trapped, the beasts pounded at the shimmering wall with their appendages, gibbering in rage. My sweat ran cold when I understood that this meant we were trapped in here with them, too. The sensation in my stomach was very much like the feeling of being stuck in a room that was slowly filling up with water, only instead of water, I was contending with a frothing mass of razor-toothed octopus mutants set on tearing me apart.

"Heads up," Bastion cried.

I stifled a gasp as he wrenched a telephone pole right out of the ground, sending it hurtling through the air like a missile, cleanly impaling five of the abominations in a single strike. It was a strange time to better understand his power, how he worked around the limitations of his range by using his magic to throw objects like projectiles, the way he might with an especially powerful invisible limb.

But it was also a reminder of how limited my own abilities were. I groped around on the ground, desperate to contribute at least in some way to the fight. My fingers closed around a lead pipe. Close enough. I wielded it like a club and charged forth, the scream coming out of my mouth sounding so far away. I was afraid, but I had to fight.

The Hands were doing the bulk of the damage, clearing out whatever else was streaming in through the portal. On the ground around us, it looked like at least fifty of the monsters had been slain, but it didn't seem like there'd be an end to the wave of horrors. Up ahead, someone screamed as one of the creatures finally found home with its tentacles. Blood pounded in my temples as I watched the thing bury its limbs in a man's chest, ripping at flesh and bone, killing him in a flurry of writhing, glistening appendages.

More yelling filled the plaza as more of the Lorica fell to the monsters. What was this all in service of? Was this the sacrifice that Thea wanted? I eyed her as she floated above the proceedings, hovering in midair like a noble watching over the peasantry. I gripped my pipe harder. She was responsible for the portal's existence. If we could take her out of the picture, even just distract her, we could loosen her hold on it, and find a way to shut it down from there.

"Thea," I screamed, my hackles rising as she turned to favor me with a slitted gaze and the smuggest of smiles. "Why are you doing this?"

She flew nearer, still infuriatingly out of reach, but close enough that I could hear her voice and her taunting.

"Call it an offering. Call it a sacrifice. Magic can only take you so far, Dustin, and what I want, only the Eldest can give."

"And what is that? Death? Mayhem? Look around you. They're destroying everything. Why do this?"

Thea's smile was angelic, so far removed from the terror and carnage around us. "Because they are the only true Gods. If I do as they ask, then they will grant me anything, even dominion over life. And death." She pursed her lips. "Magic," she repeated, as if in some sort of trance, "can only take you so far, Dustin."

Life, death? Magic had its limitations, the way the Lorica couldn't simply bring me back to my father. But then it came to me, how Thea had lied about casting a massive circle. "That's how you get an apocalypse going," she told me. The dead don't just come back – unless, perhaps, through a contract with an entity so powerful that it demanded blood on an equally massive scale.

The memory of her children. The Eldest. That was what she meant.

"That's why you're doing this," I said. "Your son, your daughter. You're trying to bring them back."

Thea's face twisted into a furious mask. "Do not speak to me of my children," she hissed. But I knew I had hit the mark. Whoever these Eldest were – whatever they were – she was only doing this to earn their favor, to resurrect her children.

"There has to be another way, Thea."

"There isn't," she snarled. "You fool. I know so much more of our world than you ever will. Don't you think I've exhausted every possibility? No. This is the only way." She lifted further off the ground, raising her head to the portal. "Fare well, Dustin. Live, if you can."

I puzzled this out for the briefest second – was she really expecting me to survive any of this? – when I realized what she meant. I narrowly dodged as another tentacle whipped past my face. Twisting from the hip, I smashed the pipe across where the creature's head would be, the nest of tentacles between its shoulders.

Upon impact, the thing gave a series of screeches from its many mouths – but it didn't go limp as I'd hoped. Three of its tentacles reached out, entangling my wrists, wrenching the pipe from out of my grasp, hurling it away. Ichor and saliva dripped from more of its tentacles as it took aim for my chest, and –

A blur of green and gold streaked across the night, shearing through the air and slicing at the monster's tentacles. I felt the appendages go limp as they were severed in a singular arc, a masterful slice that, at first, I assumed had come from Bastion. Then the blur struck again, cleaving the abomination in half, rending its torso asunder.

"Vanitas," I breathed.

The sword's voice pulsed in a corner of my mind. "You're going to get yourself killed. Idiot."

"You can call me whatever you want. How did you – "

"I don't know," he said hurriedly, repositioning himself in time to hack at another of the oncoming creatures. "Our bond, perhaps. I couldn't control it. Just came smashing out of the glass, and here I am."

"Thanks," I said, reaching for my lead pipe and diving back into the fray with Vanitas, fighting inexpertly alongside the animated sword. His scabbard joined the battle too, bluntly crushing and smashing with quiet relish. From above us

Thea bellowed her rage, whether at the sword's very existence or its ability to continue carving up her fell army, I couldn't tell.

But she wasn't finished. Thea thrust her hand at the portal, a thin ray of light emanating from her fingers. I swallowed nervously, watching as the gap widened – no, doubled in size. Fuck. Her minions flooded in faster, in greater numbers than before.

I glanced around. Even with Vanitas at my side, we couldn't hope to stop them all. Prudence was panting as she fought, her motions less fluid, driven with less power. Bastion hung back from a safe distance, swatting and sweeping at the things with a telephone pole. Romira's flames didn't burn as bright. In time I knew that Vanitas would lose momentum too. It was happening. Mages didn't draw from some limitless well of power. We were running out of ammunition.

The Hands fell back. From around us fearful screams issued from the stray normals. We were trapped under the dome, unless Odessa lifted her shield. But what good would that do? It would only send the abominations out into the city. There had to be some way I could help to stop it all. I squeezed the pipe, the metal of it rough and icy against my hand, sobering. Think, Dustin. Think.

I laughed to myself haughtily, soft and low. Step. That was all I could do, was shadowstep away and out of there. Maybe find my father, tell him there was no time to explain, then just head the fuck out of Valero as fast as we could go, before the creatures could catch up to us. But wouldn't that just be delaying the inevitable?

I hated my helplessness. I hated that my thoughts turned to running. Everyone was right. The school counsellors, dad, fuck, even Hecate, who didn't know me from Adam, read what hid in my heart. All I'd ever done was run. Turn and face the darkness, she said. Easy for her to say.

But that was all I had to do: find the nearest shadow, walk into it, and enter the Dark Room. But I would be leaving all these people behind, all of them to die, these men and women who had become my colleagues, dare I say friends. Even Vanitas, whoever, whatever he truly was.

Hah. Hecate had the truth of it all along. Even she knew that my first instinct would be to run. Here I was facing down this horde of alien death, and all I had was a lead pipe. My bones yearned for the safety of the Dark Room. All I had to do was close my eyes and open the door.

"But the door opens from both ends."

My spine shivered. I couldn't rightly tell if I'd recalled Hecate's words at that precise moment, or if she had spoken them directly into my mind, but it was starting to make sense. All this time I had been pulling on the Dark Room's door to use it as an escape hatch. What if the answer wasn't to go into the shadows, but to throw that same door open – and bring the roiling, hideous denizens of the Dark Room to this reality?

"Stand back," I shouted, dropping the pipe. The sound it made as it clanged against the asphalt was fitting. If I was wrong, this would be my death knell.

"And what the hell do you expect to do against all that?" Bastion screamed, thrusting a finger at the newest oncoming rank of creatures. A hail of pebbles flew feebly as he threw his hand out, barely denting the leathery hides of the abominations.

"Trust me on this," I shouted back, though I had no reason to trust even myself. The blistering light of the portal cast such intense brilliance across everything that all that stood before it was shadow, the entire square shrouded in a writhing, undulating mass of limbs and tentacles.

I focused on that darkness, homing in on the sensation of peeling back the veil between Here and the Dark Room, only this time, I had no intention of stepping through. Whatever dwelled in that nether place – it was time to let them out.

"Dustin, we need to get out of here," Prudence shouted, so close to my ear that it nearly broke my concentration. I shook my head. "You idiot, we need to go before – "

A black mist rose from the shadows cast against the street, climbing, at first, in thin wisps, delicate tendrils that seemed to be made of smoke, or darkness. That smoke began to stir, and to churn. Still the horrors stampeded for the living, howling, frothing. All at once the mists and shadows hardened, coalescing into a baleful, bladed solidity that glimmered like crushed velvet and gleamed with the unmistakeable sharpness of steel. Something in my chest burned, low and slow, but it built into an agony so intense, like an ember forcing its way out of my body. I clenched my fists and gritted my teeth to fight the pain, but to no avail. My heart was on fire. I threw my head back and screamed.

The shadows rose as one.

Whips and lashes burst from the ground, the insides of the Dark Room hardened in this reality into something thorny, vicious, and sharp. The Hands shouted at each other to retreat as the square transformed into a nightmare pit of writhing black appendages, all hungering to slash, flay, and shred. The shadows tore into the abominations, ripping them into rubbery strips and chunks of foul meat. Every last thing that poured out of the gateway fell in the field of black grass I had conjured from the Dark.

I was doing this. I felt every blow that struck out, every knife cut inflicted within this meadow of ebony blades. I was controlling it somehow, and the fire in my chest, the sensation of my heart being thrust into boiling oil was almost worth the grand swell of power. Something like laughter threatened to burble out of me, tearing its way out of my throat. It was just another scream.

And Thea met it with her own, her face contorted in rage. "No," she shouted. The gateway was closing. My assault had finally depleted its never-ending supply of fodder. "No."

She spread her arms to her sides, fingers splayed, the very picture of fury. The air around her shimmered as she used her gift, manipulating light to use as a weapon. Reality itself wavered as she summoned an array of massive lances around her body. There were six at first, hovering near her, like guided missiles waiting on her command. The light about her flickered, and then there were a dozen spears, then twenty, then too many too count. She pointed at me, shouting wordlessly. As one, the spears flew for my throat.

The pain in my chest was too intense, searing at my insides, rooting me to the spot. More and more spears appeared around Thea, an unending hail of javelins, like a salvo of comets waiting to annihilate me. Yet I couldn't move. If I had to die, then at least I knew I died saving the city.

Hey dad, I thought. Look. I'm a hero.

But the spears never hit home, colliding and bursting in the air just inches from my face in scintillant flashes of light. Two bodies stepped into my peripheral vision, and I knew how I had survived. To my left, Odessa had her hand out, one of her shields erected invisibly. To my right, with sweat dripping down his neck, Bastion exacted the last of his power to keep me protected.

Which left me free to focus on the only enemy we had left.

With the final dregs of my strength I forced the pulsing mass of shadow to rise from the ground, black ropes of solid darkness twisting into a singular, massive tentacle. It crashed upward, roaring like a tidal wave, reaching easily to Thea's height and driving forward with enough force to halve her at the torso in one horrible slice, or to pulverize her in a single blow. My first friend in the underground, my mentor, my murderer. Straining against the pain, I bid her a silent, remorseless goodbye.

But the blow never hit home. Thea cursed me, her teeth sharp and white, and before the surge of shadow collided with her body a blinding flash of light scorched the night. When I looked again, she was gone. With nothing left to destroy, the shadows dissipated into motes, little droplets of night returned to the blackness of the Dark Room.

"Fuck," Bastion shouted. Good old Bastion, never at a loss for words. "Fuuuck," he yelled again. "She got away." He raked at his hair in frustration, then looked left and right, at the sticky mass of severed tentacles and oozing rubbery blackness, the only signs that the children of the Eldest were ever here. "Fuck," he shouted. "Who's going to clean this up?"

It was almost funny to me, how Bastion could hardly decide whether sanitation or Thea's escape was more important, and I might have laughed if I didn't feel like my entire ribcage had been torched right out of my body. Nothing had ever been that painful to me, and I didn't understand how I had survived. The agony was subsiding, but it was dreadfully clear that calling on the Dark Room had taken something out of me.

I patted at my torso, my chest, just to be sure that I hadn't actually been burned alive. Everything was still there. My hand came away wet, though. Sopping wet, and I wondered how I could have possibly sweated so much.

"Dustin," Prudence said, running up to me. "That was incredible! How did you – Dustin, you're bleeding."

I looked at my hand. It was covered in red. I laughed.

"Oh," I said, chuckling. "Oh, good. At least I wasn't burned."

"Dustin, we need to get you out of here." Prudence's eyes were wide with terror, and I knew that I was in trouble. "We need a cleric," she shouted. "Here. Now."

How was I still alive? I held out my palm for Prudence to see, proud as I had been in first grade when I was finger-painting, when Mrs. Moyer said I showed an aptitude for art, when I knew even then that I would always like everything and never be good at anything.

But it wasn't fair. I finally found something I

could be good at. I didn't want to die. I didn't want to go. Not yet.

I touched my chest again. Under my shirt, something felt ragged, and torn, and it stung insanely. Ah. My scar, from the ritual dagger. It had reopened. I held my hand out again, up against the light blazing from the moon. The stars were singing to me. But it was too loud, and too bright.

Too bright. I needed the darkness.

"Hey dad," I said, laughing. "Look. I'm a hero."

The world went black.

Chapter 21

Everything was blinding white when I opened my eyes again. My mouth was cotton-dry, my head felt like it had been kicked in repeatedly, and my chest – the best I could say was that it felt like a small, burning coal had been shoved in there, like someone was driving a cigarette into me, right through my scar.

And somehow, in these cases, my mind had been conditioned to expect one and only one person at my bedside: Thea. I guess it was only natural for me to start scrambling against the headboard the first time I opened my eyes since the battle outside HQ. Later on I was told that I was screaming. They had to sedate me.

It turned out that it was always someone different keeping watch over me. Prudence, a few times, and Herald. Even Bastion, bless him and his douchebaggery.

Clerics took turns fixing me up, or so I was told. It wasn't a one-doctor job, and several clerics had to go through cycles of healing and expending energy, but I liked to think that I wasn't the only case they were working on. There were a lot of injuries in the aftermath of the battle at the square, after all.

Bastion tried to convince me that I was an especially tough patient to handle, though. All the screaming, he said. I scoffed at first, but Prudence later told me that I took a lot out of the clerics because my wounds weren't only physical. I didn't ask what she meant by that. All I knew was that the burning in my heart eventually subsided.

At some point, in between the marathon sleeping sessions, I noticed that a television had found its way into a corner of my room. I knew that no one had installed it, that this was HQ's way of reacting to my presence, because some part of me wanted to know what was going on. And that was how I caught up on things, in small, blurry periods of wakefulness.

Between news reports and snatches of conversation with Prudence and, once, with Odessa, I put things together in my drug and magic-addled state. Odessa's shield had done its work of locking the abominations in and keeping the normals safe.

Shrikes, the Scions had come to call them, the creatures with tentacles and dozens of mouths, the things that bayed like demons, the children of the Eldest. Then the Lorica had sent out teams of Mouths to wipe all traces of the battle from the minds of the normals and emergency responders who were within the vicinity.

It would have been too much work, no, near impossible to rectify things for the entire city, though, so those furthest from HQ, and the public, in general, were appeased with some cockamamie story about a PR stunt for an upcoming blockbuster. That was what the pillars of light and explosive battle were for, all just a roadshow for some big-ass movie with a promotional budget to match its production.

The Lorica had more than enough funds lining its coffers to get multiple PR firms and news outlets cracking on the story, enough to drum up buzz and create a cover for a film that was never going to happen. I joined the Lorica in fervently hoping that people would eventually forget about *Hypergalactic Facepuncher: Armageddon in Lunar City*.

They never found Thea. She probably blinked off somewhere to lick her wounds. I tried to take some comfort in knowing that she couldn't possibly do anything more destructive than calling that massive circle, but knowing what little I did of magic and the underground, I was sure that Valero hadn't seen the last of her.

Her shrieking portal, Prudence explained, was an actual rupture into our dimension. Not just a regular gateway, but a proper tear, the summoning circle being massive enough to have possibly caused permanent damage to our reality. The exact point of the rift became an object of curiosity for the Lorica, something that HQ's biggest brains had explained was now the brittlest part of our world.

Kind of like how scientists noticed that there was a thinning in the ozone layer before a permanent hole was punched in it. Great. Super awesome. Prudence said HQ was working on a way to reinforce the barrier, to make sure we never got another screaming tide of hell beasts ever again. The last thing we needed was another shrike invasion. I didn't like the way her eyes kept glancing away from mine when she told me about it.

Days passed – it felt like weeks, really – and my aches subsided enough that I could get around on my own again. Color me boring, but I felt that I'd had enough action for what was technically only my first month on the job. One day Odessa was visiting, and I more or less tendered my resignation by telling her I didn't think I had what it took to be a Hound anymore.

Odessa sighed. "I don't blame you. Things are never quite this dangerous at the Lorica. Haven't been for a long time, but it looks like Thea Morgana was in it for the long haul."

Morgana? That was Thea's last name? God. I really didn't know her at all.

"She really took her time to study what she needed," Odessa continued. "Fifteen years at the Lorica. Can you imagine? Waiting that long, biding her time until the right victim came along – sorry."

I gave a weak smile and tried to shrug it off. Fifteen years? That would put Odessa at ten years old when she joined the Lorica, which made no damn sense. The only thing old about the Scion was something in her eyes, a kind of depth and knowing that only came with experience and age. Maybe I'd never find out her secrets, but I still had a couple of questions that needed answering.

I was in the middle of packing my things then. Truth be told, I guess I didn't really need to tell Odessa anything about leaving the Lorica. The sight of me sorting out my belongings must have been resignation enough.

"About that. Me being the victim and everything. Is there any reason she might have picked me?"

Odessa shook her head. "I can't think of anything specific. I'm inclined to believe what Thea said, that you just happened to be there. Still, the question remains: what exactly did she do to you?"

It was my turn to shake my head. "My guess is as good as yours. Like that whole thing with the shadows just – spilling out of me. Ripping things apart."

"Yes. That. Those things on the field that night, the mists and the tentacles. Is that what you see inside your head?"

"Not in my head, but in the Dark Room, when I walk through it to step somewhere else."

Her eyes narrowed. "I don't think you need me to tell you that there were stark similarities between your shadows and the shrikes that poured out of that rift. The tentacles, I mean, the blackness. At best I can tell you that the source of Thea's battalion is the same source that feeds your very specific brand of magic."

"The Eldest." The word made me shiver. Just a word, but loaded with too much meaning I couldn't decipher or comprehend.

"Whatever it was that she embedded inside you seems to anchor your power to the Eldest and their reality. It must be why your magic is so – unusual. We've seen Wings with abilities similar to yours, but considering what you did the night of the attack – no, you aren't strictly a Hand either, are you?"

I set down a shirt, sat on the edge of the bed, and stared at my palms. "I'm not sure what I am, if I'm honest." Or what Thea had turned me into. I clenched my fists. "But whatever that is. Do you – am I going to turn into one of those things, you think? Am I one of them, whatever they are?"

Odessa pressed her lips together, then shook her head. "Unlikely. The shrikes were grunts, just minions. Your abilities are different. Stranger. More connected, I think, to the Eldest themselves."

"You're a Scion. You know more than the rest of us. What are the Eldest?" Maybe Odessa could tell me something the others hadn't.

"Well," Odessa said, folding her hands together. "You know about the entities. What Thea said was not untrue. The Eldest are the first among all. Ravenous, mindless beings that are not of this earth or this reality. And we're only better off for it."

"So where are they?"

"I can't say. A different dimension, somewhere beyond the stars. These things are so ancient that they predate mankind entirely. But their power reaches so far that even with Thea's rift closed, we have no guarantee of safety. The Eldest are primal, terrible, immense. They existed before us, and so will they remain when we're dead and gone."

We, Odessa said, which at least clued me in to how she was, in fact, human. That made one of us. It still offered no answer to what I was, or what I had become. I scratched at my chest absently and went back to packing.

"But yes. That's something to worry about another day. Whatever it is, Mr. Graves, I have every confidence that you know what you're doing now that you intend to leave the Lorica."

What a strange thing to say, I thought. I

turned to her, unsure of how to respond. Odessa's eyes gleamed with dark understanding. We were alone in that room, yet it still felt as though she wanted to keep things subtle – in case someone was watching, or listening.

"I have every confidence that you'll find the right answers," she said.

It was as if she knew exactly what I had planned, somehow, which was odd, because even I wasn't sure what I was going to do myself. I only nodded, and when she extended a hand to shake goodbye, I accepted. Her hand was warm – human – and she didn't recoil when her fingers met my palm. At least I knew I was still human, too.

Odessa left me to finish packing, but a rapping at the doorway just seconds after she departed tugged at my attention. It was Herald.

"So," he said. "You're really going."

"I really am." I shrugged. "Guess I'm not really cut out to be a Hound after all."

Herald scoffed and folded his arms. "You know that isn't true. You're going to keep in touch, right? We still get to hang out and stuff."

I frowned. "Don't be stupid. Of course we can. I've got your number and everything."

Herald nodded. He watched me for a bit in silence, then cleared his throat, nodding at my things. "You sure you've got everything?"

I raised an eyebrow. "Um, yes. I think so."

"Good thing I had a spare backpack to lend

you from the archives, then."

"Yeah," I said, looking at him with a puzzled expression. "Good thing."

I was grateful for the loaner, sure. Probably one of the most practical magical objects I'd ever seen at the Gallery, this backpack that could carry far more than its size should realistically allow. I kept dumping stuff in and it just kept taking it all, never bulging or growing in size. Herald told me that the bag was actually an opening to a pocket dimension. It really saved me the hassle of packing all of my stuff into boxes.

"Just be sure to return it once you've moved in and settled. I'll get flayed if we don't get it back." He cleared his throat and adjusted his tie. "Checked it out especially for you."

I chuckled. "Appreciate it. And yeah, I'll be sure to bring it back."

"Empty," he said. "Totally empty. Be sure you don't leave anything in there."

My forehead creased again. Herald was being weird about this, but he was doing me such a solid with this whole magical bag thing that I didn't want to be an ass about it. I said nothing and slung the backpack's straps over my shoulders. Oh, and that was the best part, too. The bag never got heavy. For all anyone knew, all I had in it were some clothes and some books. Someone could look at me and think I was just a college kid going to his next class, and not some dude hauling around an entire apartment's worth of crap. Man, I love magic.

"Looks like you're sorted then," Herald said. He waited for me to walk up to the door, then stuck a hand out.

"Aww, come on, a handshake?" I tugged on his hand, pulling him in for a hug, squeezing until I got a chortle out of him. "I'll see you around, buddy."

Herald smoothed down the creases I made in his waistcoat, then, walking backwards, smiled tightly and gave me a half-hearted salute as he headed back to the Gallery.

I plodded out into the main corridor, sneakers looking pedestrian as always against the lush carpet. I took in the paneled walls that gleamed so much I could almost make out my reflection in them. I watched as sheaves of paper flew like birds across the halls in the galleries below, because sure, email existed, and so did network servers, but this? This was all about style. I found myself sighing. I was going to miss this place.

Someone to my left cleared his throat in a, well, I could only describe it as a douchey way. This, I wasn't sure I was going to miss. Without turning, I greeted my intruder.

"Hey, Bastion," I said, with little enthusiasm in my voice.

"So," he said. "I hear you're leaving."

I hiked my backpack higher up on my shoulder and jerked my head at it. "What tipped you off?"

He was in his usual leather jacket, a pair of aviator sunglasses pushed into hair that had been deliberately mussed, to look effortless, or something. Still, my reflexive irritation didn't begin bubbling up instantly at the sight of him. Something seemed different. His posture didn't seem so rigid, not quite bent on picking a fight.

He gave me a wry smile. "You gonna miss us, aren't you?"

I scoffed. "Not you. Don't flatter yourself." I grasped the straps of my backpack, then looked over the bannister at the endless swarms of paper, at the gleaming brass fixtures, the globes of enchanted firelight, the small army of workers going about their day as if their front door hadn't recently been assaulted by a swarm of tentacled demons from beyond the stars. "This, though? Maybe. A little."

Bastion chuckled. "Yeah. It's a good place to be. Feels like you're doing something right for the world, you know?"

"Yeah," I said wistfully. Like being a hero, in some small way.

"You did good that night," Bastion said. He made a cough. "And fine, you weren't making shit up about your precious sword. Anyway. Whatever it was you did out there, it was – it was kind of awesome."

I put on my smarmiest grin, then shrugged. "Hey. You just have to trust in Dustin."

Bastion grimaced. "That was awful the first

time you tried it, Graves. It's terrible. You're terrible."

"It's not, and I'm not. And awesome's nice, but you saw what happened when I used the shadows. Damn well ripped my chest open. I don't know if I should ever try that again."

"You'll learn," he said, chucking me on the shoulder. What the hell was going on? Bastion being nice to me, just when I was leaving? Man. I wondered if we could have been friends. Maybe we were all along and I just didn't want to admit it. "Well. Whatever it is you're up to next." He held out a hand. "Good luck."

I smiled and reached for his hand. In one quick motion he withdrew it, then smoothed his hair back against his scalp.

"Psych," he muttered, strutting away.

That's more like it, I thought. Good old bad Bastion.

I said my goodbyes to anyone else I came across, most memorably Romira at reception, who either made a great show of being sorry to see me go, or genuinely had some sort of tiny crush on me.

"I'll miss you lots, Dust," she cooed, playing with her hair.

I grinned, then coughed nervously, hoping that was enough to convey that I'd miss her too, playful teasing and all. She waved one hand lazily in the direction of the front door, little wisps of fire trailing after every motion of her lacquered nails as she deactivated the traps. I smiled, tipped an invisible hat at her, and left.

It was a beautiful day out in Valero. I hadn't realized how long I'd been stuck in my room at the Lorica just recovering, and the contrast of being locked in for so long was so much more glaring now that I was outdoors. The sun was out, as was a light breeze, making everything balmy, lazy. The streets weren't packed, but the din of city life was oddly comforting, the voices of people talking to each other or into their cellphones, hip-hop and reggaeton spilling out of windows as cars drove by.

It was so good to be out, in fact, that I almost missed Prudence standing at the foot of HQ's stairs, a funny sort of smile on her face. The wind shifted her hair, revealing that little secret patch of blue at her nape.

"You're actually doing it," she said. "You're actually leaving."

I put on a sterner face than usual, maybe to disguise how this was making me sadder than I'd expected. "Come on, now. Don't make this harder than it already is."

Her smile went a little brighter. "Then I won't. But I'd be lying if I said we wouldn't miss you, Dust."

I might have blushed a little. I scratched the back of my neck. "I mean, it's not like I'm moving away or anything." How did I know that? I had no way of saying just yet. "We can meet up for coffee some time. Do lunch."

"I'd like that. I'll cut you a deal. You buy lunch, and I don't bring Bastion."

I laughed. "That honestly sounds like a bargain."

"So. I hate to phrase it like this because it's just so – ugh – corporate, but where are you going now?" She tilted her head, studying me. "What's next for you?"

I tilted my head too, mirroring her, suddenly struck by exactly where I meant to go. I grinned.

"I have a few ideas."

Chapter 22

But first, unfinished business. Backpack strapped to my shoulders, a plastic bag in my hand, I stared at my father's front door. It had been months since I'd stood there in broad daylight. I bit my lip. Part of me considered running away.

No, I told myself. This was what needed to be done. No more running. I had to tell him everything, from what happened the night I disappeared, all the way to the night I may or may not have helped save the world, or at least, the city. At the very least I wanted him to know that I kept a stable job for longer than a month. But again, yes, the saving the world bit.

Beads of water dripped from the plastic bag onto the cracked cement of the house's front porch. I'd picked up a few beers along the way –

not to encourage my dad's habit, no, but because it was part of our ritual, part of how we bonded.

I lifted my hand, knuckles poised to rap on the door, when I stopped. Was this actually the right thing to do? Would he even acknowledge me? How would he react knowing that I was supposed to be dead?

"Go to him," Sterling had said. He was right. It didn't matter for as long as I could tell dad everything that happened. He'd believe me, and he'd understand. I sucked in a lungful of air, my chest puffing out. He'd be proud of what I'd done. Finally, he'd be proud.

Kind of weird taking advice from a vampire, I know, and weirder still acknowledging that vampires were now a part of my existence, but Sterling had the right idea. I wrinkled my forehead, straightened my back, and knocked loudly, three times.

Couldn't help it. I grinned widely, something loosening inside of me, my chest expanding at the very thought that I was going to see my dad again, that there was a chance we could rebuild our relationship and carry on like the good old times.

I glanced over my shoulder, at the lawn where I used to play as a kid that had now gone brown and bone-dry. I could help him with that. We could sort that all out in time, nurture the grass as we nurture our relationship. We could go to the sea like we used to, do one of those picnics in the sand and talk about mom. I missed the ocean. I missed her.

But a minute had passed, and nothing. Maybe – maybe he was asleep, I considered. I knocked again, five times, louder this time. He couldn't be at work. It was a Saturday. Stupid me, though. What if he was out doing groceries, or seeing some friends? Yeah, that was it.

I walked around to the side of the house, in full view, this time, of the large window where I used to peek in to watch him by night. I wasn't sure what I was expecting to find. Bottles strewn across the kitchen table, maybe, boxes of day-old pizza or Chinese food that he'd taken to leaving out since I'd left. But the kitchen was clean. Not just clean, though. Everything was gone.

My heart pounded as I pressed up against the glass. The refrigerator, the kitchen table, even that dried-up plant by the doorway to the living room, all gone. I gritted my teeth. Where was he?

My gaze focused on my own shadow, cast across the floor from the sunlight streaming in through the window. In half a second I had shadowstepped into the house. It smelled musty, like it hadn't been aired out in weeks, maybe months. Motes of dust hung in the air, floating peacefully like little creatures, like the only things left living in this place.

I rushed to the living room. The couch, the television, the coffee table, all of them, gone. Pictures of my dad, of my mom, of me, none of them were there. All gone.

Something like loss twisted in my chest. Sterling had been right all along. I choked. I wanted to tell myself it was the dust, but I knew that it wasn't.

"Dad?"

I let my feet carry me up the stairs to the bedrooms, where I knew I would find nothing. The bed frames lingered, the mattresses either moved or sold off. I bit my lip.

Glass tinkled. I wasn't sure when the plastic bag had slipped from my fingers, but amber liquid crept slowly across the floor, pooling around my feet. I clenched my fists.

"Dad?" I said again, hoping that someone would answer.

No one did.

Chapter 23

"This is great."

I shoveled another helping of chicken straight into my mouth, chasing it with a heap of white rice. The meat was cooked in a dark sauce, tangy, sour, rich. Couldn't get enough of it.

Gil nodded in silent approval. Sterling looked on with a tired, glazed expression, and Carver hid his smile behind steepled fingers, watching me over the gleaming perfection of his buffed nails.

I kept going for more, attacking my plate like I hadn't eaten in days. "What did you say this was again?" I said, through a mouthful of rice.

Sterling raised an eyebrow. "Chicken adobo. It's Filipino food. You know, like the sign outside says."

"No need to get snippy," I said, maybe a little

too sulkily. "It was just a question." And I had many, many more.

It wasn't hard to find these guys. Rather, it wasn't hard for them to find me. All I had to do was sit alone out in the open where I was vulnerable and exposed to danger. Naturally, I picked Heinsite Park, the very place where I was abducted shortly before being sacrificed, and, incidentally, the same park where Sterling and Gil had chased me. I kept glancing at my watch to see how long it would take for one of them to show up. Ten minutes, almost on the dot, and Sterling had slunk up next to me on the park bench, a cigarette dangling from his thin, bloodless lips.

"I'm ready to talk," I told him. And he took me to this Filipino place, a little restaurant just on the edge of the Meathook. Calling it a restaurant was generous, really, considering it only had four tables, plastic chairs to sit at, and kind of grimy linoleum flooring. The fluorescent lighting really emphasized just how pale I'd always thought Sterling was, except it turned out that he was even more pallid than that. Gil looked like just another guy off the street, albeit a really tall, muscular, and somewhat hairy one.

And Carver? As out of place as he was in a grubby restaurant wearing his finely tailored suit, he looked like a million bucks, with the manicured beard, the gems gleaming from every finger, his eyebrows angled in a way that expressed both curiosity and cockiness. Like Sterling, he'd healed all his injuries perfectly, despite claiming not to be a vampire. Hmm. Curiouser and curiouser.

There was Mama Rosa too, who I assumed was the owner of the place. Kind of a no-brainer, I guess, considering it was called Mama Rosa's Fine Filipino Food. She was a hulking woman, with fists like hams, a face like a bulldog, and a ferocity to match. I hadn't heard her speak a single word the entire time she served us, but she stood behind the counter with a grim expression, a cigarette tucked behind one ear, clearly listening to everything we said. I put on a smile to try and disarm her – not for any friendliness, but because we all know I have a pathological need to feel liked – but her stony veneer barely cracked.

I polished off the adobo, then stared longingly at my empty plate, strongly considering asking for seconds. Even knowing that Carver and the others seemed to be on friendly terms with Mama Rosa, I had a hunch that they wouldn't try to poison me. Every last one of those four people in that restaurant, even Rosa – especially Rosa – could have easily killed me. I didn't stand a chance, and they knew it, and they wouldn't have had to resort to poison to do that.

"Mr. Graves is right, Sterling," Carver said in a voice like spiced honey. "It was only a question, after all." The corner of his mouth quirked. "And I'm certain he has many, many more."

He could read my mind, I was almost sure of it. But whatever. Even if he could, that'd only make it easier to sort everything out.

"So," I started. "You said that you knew what I was."

Carver shrugged. "Not everything has to have a name."

"But you're a werewolf," I said, nodding at Gil. He nodded back. "And you're a vampire." Sterling shrugged. "And you?"

Carver smiled, and spread both his hands. "The same as you. Or different, perhaps. Unique." His chair scraped against the linoleum as he stood. The other two followed suit. "Come. You should see your new home."

"Home?" I quirked an eyebrow, standing myself as I picked up my backpack.

"I give my associates living quarters. It's safer for – for people like us."

Reflexively, I reached for my wallet, nodding at Mama Rosa. Her expression remained unchanged.

"There's really no need," Carver said. "It's on the house. Mama Rosa's happy enough that you liked her cooking."

I cast her another glance. She didn't look happy at all. Matter of fact, she kind of looked like she wanted to rip my head off with her bare hands. Maybe that was just part of her charm. I followed as Carver, Sterling, and Gil headed to the kitchen.

"Uh, exit's that way," I said.

They ignored me. I shrugged. We walked a short way into the kitchen, Mama Rosa still stood up front, arms folded like a bouncer. We stopped by an industrial refrigerator.

I chuckled and rapped my knuckles against the patch of exposed brick wall right by it. "What is this, like, a secret door?"

Carver said nothing. Sterling frowned at me, his lip curled in an irritated sneer. "Dude. Just. Shut up, okay? Just watch."

And so I did, keeping my teeth clenched the whole while. Carver drew a circle in midair, and I held my breath as his fingers left a trail of amber fire. He slid one finger across one of his many rings, which had a protuberant, tiny blade that I hadn't noticed. A bead of blood formed at the tip of his finger. Sterling, I noticed, licked his lips.

The ring of fire settled into the brick wall, scorching a circle there. Carver pressed his bloodied finger against the brick. The crimson of his blood disappeared into the wall, and all at once the bricks slid apart, vanishing into nothingness, replaced by a shimmering, amber portal, orange like Carver's eyes.

Sterling stepped through nonchalantly. Without giving me a second glance, Carver stepped into the portal as well, his body disappearing into the orange glow. I looked over my shoulder in confusion. Mama Rosa was at the till, counting out the day's earnings. A hand pressed against my back.

"Get in," Gil said gruffly.

Too late to run, I thought, but again, if these people wanted me dead, they could have done that earlier, and in very many, very creative ways. Fine. I pulled on my straps, walked through –

And found myself in a great hall made of the palest, smoothest stone. Thick, featureless pillars ran the length of it, hewn out of the same rock as the perfect floor. Golden-amber light spilled from fires I couldn't see, hidden cleverly in alcoves between the columns. There was no ceiling, or if it was there, it was so high up since all I could spot was inky blackness.

Gil nudged me forward again, gently, but firmly. I walked along, too stunned to protest. What the hell was this? Carver kept his hideout in the back of some Filipino restaurant out by the Meathook?

Several feet along we met up with Carver and Sterling, who had stopped just in front of a stone formation. No, it was a statue, I could tell, but all I could see of it was its knees, as huge as it was, stretching up into the darkness. Gil fell into step with the rest of us, looking as unperturbed as Sterling by the sight of what looked to me to be the inside of some massive, ancient temple.

"You cast a circle to get us in here," I said.

"Correct," Carver said patiently.

"I thought only gods could do that." I made no effort to hide my shock. "Keep realms and domiciles, I mean."

"Maybe I am a god."

My mouth fell open. That would explain so much. "Are you?"

Carver shrugged. "Who can say?" I looked to Sterling and Gil, who said nothing.

"Rooms to your left," Sterling said wearily. "Yours is the last in the hall. Go get settled." He turned to Carver. "If you don't need me for the rest of the night, I'm gonna go look for food."

Yikes. Food? Carver nodded wordlessly.

"I'll come with," Gil said. "Nice night out."

I wondered if that meant that he was going to hunt, too. What did werewolves eat, anyway? I shuddered to think. The two of them headed back down the hall and out of the shimmering amber portal we had entered through, which I now saw was suspended precisely between the outstretched arms of two disturbingly lifelike statues of human skeletons.

Carver pointed to the right of the massive statue we were standing next to. "My office is down that way. I'd like you to come and see me once you get settled. I trust you'll find your accommodations suitable, but feel free to tell me if there's anything else you'll need."

I nodded and we headed in opposite directions. If I didn't have any context Carver could have sounded just like the night manager at some really fancy – and really niche – hotel, but it made me consider my position when I realized he was being so, well, hospitable. Too hospitable, maybe?

There were precisely three doors in the hallway I'd been asked to go down. The first was shut. The second was closed, too, and had a sign on the knob that said "Keep out!" in bold red letters, the kind of thing a teenager would hang on their bedroom door. I snickered, positive that it was Sterling's room. The final room's door was ajar. I had to restrain a gasp when I got there.

The room was brightly lit with incandescent lights fixed into the ceiling, and a couple of quite contemporary-looking lamps. Approximately everything was hewn from stone – the makeshift desk, the side tables to either side of the bed, even the empty set of shelves that looked perfect for displaying books, or knickknacks.

There was a loose assortment of tasteful furniture for the bits that wouldn't have been practical if made from stone, like the cabinets and the swivel chair by the desk, or the very plush-looking couch and carpet. The room even had an ample amount of electrical outlets, ready for someone to plug in a phone charger. I wasn't wrong about my initial assumption: this may as well have been a suite in some really luxe and really specific hotel. The mattress was plush, too, the kind you wanted to just lie in forever. It was easily the nicest room I'd ever get to live in.

The thought gave me pause. I was, quite basically, sleeping with the enemy. I knew it looked like this was me consorting with the Bad Guys, but come on. Considering what I'd gone through with Thea, there truly was no telling who was who anymore. Where was I meant to draw the line between good and evil? Everything looked better in gray, as far as I was concerned, and working with Carver meant getting answers, more, at least, than I was getting from Thea and the Lorica.

Plus I had an inkling that Carver wouldn't be the type to turn around and sacrifice his employees at a moment's notice. Call it a hunch. Gil didn't look too bad, either. Quiet guy, but he seemed pretty decent. Of course, I had no real experience of how he might behave during a full moon, but hey, I liked to believe in the best in people.

Sterling could get annoying at times, but nothing worse than Bastion, and I knew I could handle that. Only real problem would be if he had any habit of creeping into people's rooms to suck their blood at night. My hand went to my throat reflexively, and I checked on the door. Ah, a lock on the knob, and a sliding bolt. Good. Whatever else Carver was, it looked like he at least respected privacy.

Unpacking was uneventful, and Herald's magical bag of magic spat out my belongings in the reverse order of how I had put them in. Soon I had everything sorted into the cabinets and onto the stone shelves. I stood with my hands at my hips, proud that I had managed to fit my entire life into this fancy shmancy bedroom.

I dipped my hand into the backpack again, just to make sure I'd gotten everything, but as I groped around, my fingers made contact with something unfamiliar. The hairs at the back of my neck prickled. What the hell was this long, heavy thing? Had Herald forgotten something in there? Or – wait. Had he intended for me to find it all along?

I pulled out the object – the sword – and grinned, beside myself with excitement.

"Vanitas," I muttered. Hot damn, Herald. What a parting gift.

"Graves," the sword said, a rumble of contentment in his telepathic voice.

"I was wondering why Herald so violently wanted me to turn this backpack inside out."

"Yeah. Bit stuffy in there. Put me somewhere I can air out, will you?"

"You don't breathe."

"And you don't know what it's like being pressed up against all your underwear." The sword gave a little huff. "Honestly, Dustin, how many pairs of boxers do you need?"

"Yeah, I missed you too, buddy."

I gave Vanitas his own place of honor on an empty stone shelf. He looked impressive there, the greenish-gold of his tarnish glowing eerily in the lamplight.

"Catch up later," I said. "Gotta go talk things

out with my new boss."

Vanitas didn't answer, but I heard a mild scraping as he shifted on the shelf, apparently already getting comfortable with his new surroundings.

I made my way back down the hall, passed the giant statue, and entered another corridor much like the one housing our quarters. This one had no doors to either side, though, just more pillars and hidden lights. My footsteps rang into the vast emptiness of the strange dimension, the sound of them fading into nothingness.

At the end, the corridor opened up into a massive room, so huge that I couldn't see the walls, the floors just stretching out into void. In the middle sat Carver, at an impressive stone desk set with amber jewels. Two ornately carved wooden chairs sat across his desk, each finished with lush scarlet upholstery. He gestured at one of them as he saw me approaching, beckoning me to take a seat.

"So," he said. "How is your room?"

I patted at the velvet cushion before I sat, relishing the plushness of it under my fingers. "Sumptuous. I swear I've never used that word before today, but, wow."

Carver smiled. "I'm glad you like it." He cracked his knuckles, unconsciously, it seemed, and I realized for the first time that he wasn't wearing a black glove. I opened my mouth to remark on it, but Carver picked up right away.

"For the last time, there is no such thing as a – what did you call it again? A Black Hand?"

"Yes. That."

He scoffed. "There's never been an organization of that name. Your former mentor used that to deceive you."

I nodded at his hand. "So what about the glove, then?"

"I thought it looked stylish," Carver said coldly. He drew his hand back, as if stung, and his lip twitched with just the barest hint of hurt. "Never mind all that. Now, to business. You will receive a salary for the services you will render under my employ, which will not be dissimilar to the work you did for the Lorica."

"Much appreciated," I said, unsure of whether I should try to negotiate. We hadn't discussed numbers, but something about Carver's accommodations and the nature of his domicile, if it could be called that, told me that he wasn't a stingy man.

"I understand that you will want to locate your father. I can make no promises, but I will attempt to assist you in divining his whereabouts as well as I can."

"I – wow. Thank you. And to think that before all this I thought you guys just wanted me dead."

Carver's smile shifted into something else, the quirk of his lip wry. "And to think that you tried to destroy me with your bottled lightning."

Blood rushed to my face, and I wondered if he

could see me blush in the strange lighting of his not-office. "Sorry about that. Like I said, I thought you guys were gonna kill me."

"Water under the bridge," he said, waving a hand dismissively. "In truth I appreciate the quick thinking. I understand those bottles were never meant for combat purposes, eh? Shows you have an ability to improvise."

Or, truthfully, that I had an ability to panic and throw shit at people when I was scared. But I didn't say any of that out loud, and just nodded.

"Now," Carver said, folding his hands together. "Before we proceed. Do you have any questions?" He held up a finger. "Apart from the notion of what you are. That answer will come in time, as we grow to learn more of the Eldest."

I chewed my lip. I really only had one thing to ask. "What are you?" I said, shortly before realizing how rude that might sound. Too late to take it back.

Carver watched me over the steeples of his fingers for a long, uncomfortable moment. Nothing in the temple made a single sound.

"I am like you, in that I am also endowed with magical ability," he said slowly. "Call me a sorcerer, if you will. The only difference is that I am older than many you may have met. As I'm sure you've come to learn, it is study and time that allows a mage to truly unlock his potential."

He set his hands across his desk, palms pressed down into the smooth stone. "I have found ways to extend my life beyond the bounds of mortal years. Several times over. I have, in a way, cheated death. Perhaps that is why others are unhappy with me, and consider me some kind of abomination." He chuckled.

Cheated death. I thought of Thea and how that had been her goal, finding detours around mortality, finding some method, no matter the cost, of bringing her children back. For the briefest moment I found myself sympathizing with my murderer, and for the briefest moment my mind flashed with anger.

"Beyond material gain, beyond my protection, knowledge is what you stand to earn by being under my employ," Carver continued. "For as long as you work with me, I promise to further your study in the arcane arts, to show you the things your erstwhile mentor never taught you." He leaned back, raising his nose only the slightest. "I will show you how to control the darkness that lives inside your very bones."

My mouth was dry. "I would like that very much."

Slowly, painfully slowly, the smile crept its way back to Carver's lips. "Then it's settled. Accept my offer, and you begin your apprenticeship." He extended one hand, the jewels on his fingers gleaming in the magical firelight. "Dustin Graves. Are you ready to start your life anew?"

I took his hand.

Need to read more?

Join Dustin Graves and his sentient sword Vanitas on an impromptu evening mission to stop a ritual sacrifice. Get your free copy of *Crystal Brawl* at **www.nazrinoor.com**.

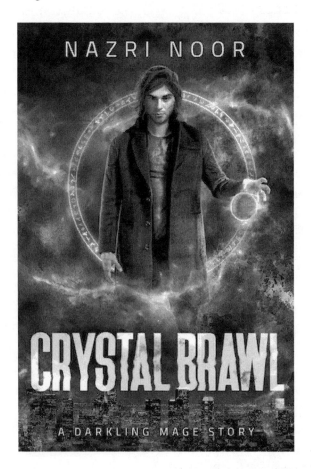

About the Author

Hi, I'm Nazri, a Filipino-Malaysian author based in California. I'm trilingual, but I really only write in English. I can also speak just enough Sindarin and Valyrian to impress absolutely no one. My urban fantasy novels focus on heroes who use wits, style, and their wildly unpredictable magic to save the day. Think sass and class, while kicking ass.

My influences come from horror and fantasy: HP Lovecraft, Anne Rice, George R.R. Martin, Chuck Palahniuk, Terry Pratchett, and Neil Gaiman. Growing up I was shaped by the *Blood Sword*, *Fighting Fantasy*, *Lone Wolf*, and *Grey Star* game book universes. I'm also inspired by video games, specifically the *Castlevania*, *Final Fantasy*, and *Persona* series.

Long story short, I'm a huge nerd, and the thrill of imagining wizards and monsters and worlds into existence is what makes me feel most alive. Writing, to me, is magic. If you enjoyed my work, please do consider leaving me a review. Thank you for reading, and thank you for supporting independent authors everywhere.

To see more of my books, follow me on social media, or simply say hello, visit me online at **www.nazrinoor.com**.

Made in the USA
Middletown, DE
16 December 2021